Young and Famous

DANIEL and SUSAN COHEN

AN ARCHWAY PAPERBACK
Published by POCKET BOOKS • NEW YORK

The authors would like to thank the agents, managers, and families of many of the young stars who helped us obtain information and photographs for this book. We note, however, that these are not authorized biographical sketches.

Cover photograph of Rob Lowe by Vinnie Zuffante/Star File
Cover photograph of Michael J. Fox by George Lange/Outline

AN ARCHWAY PAPERBACK *Original*

An Archway Paperback published by
POCKET BOOKS, a division of Simon & Schuster, Inc.
1230 Avenue of the Americas, New York, N.Y. 10020

Copyright © 1987 by Daniel Cohen and Susan Cohen

All rights reserved, including the right to reproduce this book or portions thereof in any form whatsoever. For information address Pocket Books, 1230 Avenue of the Americas, New York, N.Y. 10020

ISBN: 0-671-63493-3

First Archway Paperback printing February 1987

10 9 8 7 6 5 4 3 2 1

AN ARCHWAY PAPERBACK and colophon are registered trademarks of Simon & Schuster, Inc.

Printed in the U.S.A.

IL 4+

Meet the *young* and *famous:*

Molly Ringwald
Rob Lowe
Demi Moore
Michael J. Fox
Laura Dern
Emilio Estevez
Lisa Bonet
Tom Cruise
Alyssa Milano
Ralph Macchio
Ally Sheedy
Anthony Michael Hall
Phoebe Cates
And More!

Get an inside look at the hottest young stars in Hollywood and on TV. Filled with photographs as well as the most up-to-the-minute information, *YOUNG AND FAMOUS* tells you all you've ever wanted to know about the most talked-about performers of the eighties.

Books by Daniel Cohen

GHOSTLY TERRORS
THE GREATEST MONSTERS IN THE WORLD
HORROR IN THE MOVIES
THE MONSTERS OF STAR TREK
MONSTERS YOU NEVER HEARD OF
REAL GHOSTS
SCIENCE FICTION'S GREATEST MONSTERS
STRANGE AND AMAZING FACTS ABOUT
  STAR TREK
SUPERMONSTERS
THE WORLD'S MOST FAMOUS GHOSTS

Books by Daniel and Susan Cohen

HEROES OF THE CHALLENGER
THE KID'S GUIDE TO HOME COMPUTERS
ROCK VIDEO SUPERSTARS
ROCK VIDEO SUPERSTARS II
WRESTLING SUPERSTARS
WRESTLING SUPERSTARS II
YOUNG AND FAMOUS

Available from ARCHWAY paperbacks

Most Archway Paperbacks are available at special quantity discounts for bulk purchases for sales promotions, premiums or fund raising. Special books or book excerpts can also be created to fit specific needs.

For details write the office of the Vice President of Special Markets, Pocket Books, 1230 Avenue of the Americas, New York, New York 10020.

Contents

To Be Young and Famous	1
Molly Ringwald	5
Michael J. Fox	14
Ally Sheedy	26
Tom Cruise	37
Demi Moore	48
Rob Lowe	54
Laura Dern	61
Ralph Macchio	68
Phoebe Cates	75
Anthony Michael Hall	82
Emilio Estevez	87
Alyssa Milano	94
Scott Grimes	100
The Cosby Kids	104
Lisa Bonet	104
Malcolm-Jamal Warner	108
Tempestt Bledsoe	111
Keshia Knight Pulliam	113
Young Stars from Britain	115
Helena Bonham Carter	116
Daniel Day Lewis	119
Margi Clark and Alexandra Pigg	120
About the Authors	122

INTRODUCTION

TO BE YOUNG AND FAMOUS

How would you like to make well over a million dollars for just a few months' work? Michael J. Fox can do that.

How would you like to be featured on the cover of America's leading news magazine before you were eighteen? That happened to Molly Ringwald.

How would you like to go right from high school to being a top star on the most popular television show in America? That happened to Lisa Bonet.

These are just some of the things that have happened to the young and famous actors and actresses whose lives and careers we are going to look at in this book. Of course, it isn't all glamour, either. The very bright and very outspoken young British actress, Helena Bonham

Carter, hates the word *glamour*. She doesn't like being called pretty, either (though she most certainly is). She doesn't even like being called an actress because "it stresses the female bit rather than the acting."

The acting. When you come right down to it, all of the people in this book are actors or (with apologies to Ms. Bonham Carter) actresses. There is a lot of glory in being a celebrated superstar. There's money, limousines, and hordes of fans asking for your autograph. But in the end you have to act, and acting, whether it is in films, on television, or on the stage, is hard work. It takes lots of discipline and energy.

After two back to back films and an off-Broadway show, Ralph Macchio worked himself right into a case of pneumonia.

Some of these actors and actresses, like Laura Dern and Emilio Estevez, come from families in which one or both parents were actors. They had a head start. Others, like Tom Cruise, seemed to come out of nowhere, and simply bowled people over with their talent.

While it's great to be young and famous, no one stays young forever. All young actors and actresses have to spend a lot of time carefully planning their futures.

We are going to look at the lives and careers of some of Hollywood's newest superstars (with a brief glance at some of Britain's new

To Be Young and Famous

young superstars as well). We're going to tell you who they are, where they came from, what they're doing, and what they're planning to do. We're going to tell you how it feels to be young and famous.

MOLLY RINGWALD

What do Samantha Baker, Claire Standish, and Andie Walsh have in common? They're all movie characters created by Molly Ringwald. Films like *Sixteen Candles, The Breakfast Club,* and *Pretty in Pink* have established Molly as one of Hollywood's leading stars. At age eighteen she's also one of the youngest. Molly attended high school at the Lycée Français in Los Angeles, graduating last spring.

To a lot of teenage girls Molly isn't just a star, she's an idol. With her Valley Girl style of talking and her eye for trendsetting clothes, California-born Molly has spawned a mass of imitators and look alikes dubbed Ringlets. Molly types have even begun showing up on television commercials aimed at teens. Like Molly herself, Ringlets have dyed orange-red hair and lips coated thickly with color. Of course, styles can and do change and one of these days Molly Ringwald may let her hair return to its natural dark brown shade. Nobody lately this side of Madonna has had such a loyal following of fans.

The one thing about Molly that's hard to imitate is her talent. The girl's loaded with it. See a Molly Ringwald movie and you'll notice instantly what a wonderfully expressive face she has as she tosses off lines of dialogue with skill and flair. Besides knowing how to act, Molly knows how to sing. So far she hasn't had much of a chance to show off her gifts as a vocalist in films. It seems a shame. Music just may be the most important thing in Molly's life. After all, she was born into a musical family.

Molly's father, Bob Ringwald, is a jazz pianist who's been blind since the age of ten. There are any number of fine musicians who are blind and Bob Ringwald never let his handicap get in his way. He was leader of the Great Pacific Jazz Band well before Molly was born. Other than having a father in show biz, how has music affected Molly's life? Well, when she was four years old she was already belting out songs into a microphone while audiences cheered and the Great Pacific Jazz Band played. She still enjoys singing at her father's gigs.

At age six she made an album called *Molly Sings*. In second grade her heroine was the

Molly Ringwald
(Cliff Lipson/Retna Ltd.)

great blues singer Bessie Smith, and Molly once even arrived at a school party dressed up to look like Bessie. To this day Molly can tell you all about blues, jazz—she buys records by the bunch. She's also a rock fan. One of her favorite artists is Bruce Springsteen. Her mother, Adele Ringwald, loves music, too. A lot of music spills out of the modest, unglamorous-looking Ringwald house in the San Fernando Valley where Molly lives with her mother, father, sister, brother, and three dogs. When he's not playing music, Bob Ringwald runs a restaurant and snack shop in Van Nuys. Beth Ringwald, three years older than her sister, Molly, works for A&M Records. Molly's brother, Kelly, who's only a year older than the family superstar, is a computer major at Cal State in Northridge.

When did Molly's acting career start? It began about the same time she started singing with her father's jazz band. She was four when she first appeared in an amateur production in Sacramento, the city where the Ringwalds lived before they moved to Los Angeles. Her first professional appearance was in a play by Truman Capote called *The Grass Harp*. She was five at the time. Molly was a guest star on "The New Mickey Mouse Club" on television when she was eight. In 1977, she was one of the

Molly Ringwald

orphans in a West Coast production of the musical *Annie*.

What at first seemed a triumph, landing an ongoing role in the sitcom "The Facts of Life," became a major disappointment when Molly was cut from the series after a year. But she sharpened her skills in guest spots on television shows like "Diff'rent Strokes"; an interview on the "The Merv Griffin Show" was also a career plus. Once into her teens, Molly appeared in two made-for-TV movies, *Packin' It In* and *P.K. and the Kid*.

So far so good, but Molly needed a breakaway film to set her apart from other young actresses. She got her wish when she was cast in the 1982 Columbia Pictures film *Tempest,* written and directed by Paul Mazursky. It was a serious movie starring acclaimed actor John Cassavetes. Since Molly had to play a girl from Manhattan, she and her parents moved to New York briefly so Molly could get a sense of what life in the Big Apple was like. Critics loved Molly's performance in *Tempest* and she received a Golden Globe Award nomination.

Perhaps the best thing that happened to Molly, thanks to *Tempest,* was catching the eye of a Chicago screenwriter named John Hughes. Hughes had written a script for a movie called *Sixteen Candles* and he needed a star. One look at Molly on screen and he knew he had found just the right girl to play Samantha Baker.

Sixteen Candles was one of the big hits of 1984. The movie is pure Hollywood fantasy, which means it has a wildly happy ending. But for all its comedy and wish fulfillment, it hits kids where they live. The teen years can be tough and *Sixteen Candles* captured what most kids go through. As your ordinary everyday high school sophomore, Sam (Samantha's nickname) Baker, is neither beautiful nor popular. What's more, her parents have forgotten that it's her sixteenth birthday. If that's not trouble enough, Sam is madly in love with a terrific-looking senior played by Michael Schoeffling, but is pursued instead by a mere freshman called the Geek, played by Anthony Michael Hall. Squirming with embarrassment, bubbling with happiness, or looking so down she might be ready to burst into a Bessie Smith blues song, Molly as Sam is every teenage girl rolled into one. When Sam's dream comes true at the end of *Sixteen Candles* and she wins the boy she loves, audiences of teenage girls may feel their dreams have come true, too.

Molly was praised for her performance in Hughes's next movie, *The Breakfast Club*. In contrast to *Sixteen Candles*, *The Breakfast Club* has its grim revealing moments. Five teenagers are thrown together serving detention on a Saturday afternoon. There's a jock played by Emilio Estevez, a punk played by Judd Nelson, a brain played by Anthony Michael Hall, a weirdo played by Ally Sheedy, and wealthy and popular princess Claire Standish, played by Molly Ringwald. At first, the teenagers are wary of each other and hostile. But as the day goes on, they stop pretending and express their real feelings. In the end, they learn that everybody's a bit of a brain, a rebel, a princess, a jock, and a weirdo. Molly and Judd, who are miles apart at the beginning of the movie, wind up together. What makes their relationship especially meaningful is that they are two people who would never even speak to each other walking down the hall at school. They are from different cliques, which in high school is as good as being from different worlds.

Pretty in Pink with Andrew McCarthy and Jon Cryer, sent Molly's career into higher orbit. Basically similar to *Sixteen Candles,* the movie's about senior Andie Walsh, a poor girl snubbed by the rich kids in her school. In love with a rich boy, but again pursued by a geek, she gets what she wants at last at her senior prom. By the way, pink is the key color used in the decor of Molly's real bedroom at home.

As to future film plans, Molly has her choice of dozens of scripts. She's been working with producer Warren Beatty on a comedy called

The Pickup Artist. On the horizon is a movie version of an off-Broadway play. Neither one is a teenage movie, but Molly has been urged to seek more mature roles. Still, the trio of Hughes-Ringwald movies has been so successful, who can say whether there might not be a fourth one in the offing? Molly was also scheduled to open on the New York stage, playing the title role in *Lily Dale,* by playwright Horton Foote. Fans may even find the former orphan in *Annie* starring in a Broadway musical. One of Molly's long-term goals is to make a movie about Edie Sedgwick, a celebrity in the sixties who led a tragic life. It's a role with strong dramatic possibilities.

How does Molly keep busy when she's not working? Well, there's the endless listening to music, of course, and she likes to read. Authors who rate high on Molly's list are J. D. Salinger, F. Scott Fitzgerald, and Virginia Woolf. Then there's time spent with friends. Some are kids she's known since elementary school. Some are young performers she's met through acting classes. She's especially close to rock musician Frank Zappa's children, Dweezil and Moon Unit. Maybe you caught their stint on MTV. One of the favorite places to hang out for the Ringwald crowd is Du-par's, a restaurant in Studio City. Another place popular with Molly

Molly Ringwald

is Disneyland. That's understandable for a fan of "The New Mickey Mouse Club."

Molly enjoys driving her white BMW, going shopping for clothes, using a video camera, and taking trips abroad. And, oh yes, she sees a lot of movies, old and new. After all, next to music the second most important thing in the life of the top teenage movie star in America just has to be films.

MICHAEL J. FOX

If someone asked you to name the single hottest young star around, your best bet would be to answer Michael J. Fox. If you were asked to explain why you chose Michael J. Fox, here are some very good reasons. Who else is a top film star and the star of a top-rated weekly television series? Not since the heyday of John Travolta has an actor managed to combine both careers at the same time. Every week millions of viewers watch Michael in the role of Alex Keaton on "Family Ties" on NBC and every week Michael receives over twenty-one thousand fan letters. No one else working in television in America gets as many. Michael also received a 1986 Emmy for his performance on "Family Ties."

As to his film career, is there a kid around who hasn't seen Michael play teenager Marty

(Photo: Rob Lewine, 1985; courtesy Ryder Public Relations)

McFly in *Back to the Future*? *Teen Wolf,* which seemed to be about a werewolf but was really about accepting yourself as you are, was a low-budget film made for a mere three million dollars. Though three million dollars sounds like a lot of money, when it comes to making movies it's a measly sum. When the movie opened, it made more than thirty-three million dollars and has continued to be a winner.

Salaries can be revealing, too. For *Back to the Future* Michael is believed to have received about $250,000. Since *Back to the Future,* Michael has been able to command one and a half million dollars per picture. Pepsi, which shells out a fortune to have big name stars appear in its commercials, has used Michael, along with top performers like Michael Jackson and Lionel Richie.

Behind all this glittering success and dazzling dollar signs, is a likable actor who's only five feet four and who weighs only one hundred and twenty pounds. When he got his Emmy he shouted, "I feel like I'm four feet tall!" He has sandy-colored hair, blue eyes, and is attractive although not wildly handsome. At age twenty-five, he can easily pass for sixteen. When Michael was a kid, he worried about his height but never allowed being short to really get in his way. He has a few scars from playing ice hockey, a sport he started playing when he was

Michael J. Fox

six and kept right on playing until he was sixteen. By then, most of his teammates were a good eight inches taller than he was. But that didn't stop him. Michael's latest foray into athletics is working with free weights.

Michael J. (his real middle name is Andrew; he adopted the J in honor of actor Michael J. Pollard, whom he admires) Fox was born in Edmonton, Canada. There were five children in the Fox family and Michael was fourth. His father, Bill Fox, was a career officer in the Canadian Army who retired in 1972. The family then moved to Burnaby, a suburb of Vancouver on the West Coast of Canada. Until they settled in Burnaby, the Foxes moved around quite a bit. That's usual for an army family. Michael's parents still live in Burnaby. Bill Fox works as a police dispatcher and his wife, Phyllis, is a payroll clerk. Michael has remained very close to them. His special gift to them on their thirty-fifth wedding anniversary was a trip to Europe. He's also close to the friends he made back in the days when he lived in Burnaby, and even named his pet dog, a pit bull, after the town he used to call home.

Back in Burnaby, Michael's first ambition was to become a rock musician. Maybe that's why even though the rock 'n' roll scenes in *Back to the Future* were pre-recorded by studio musicians, Michael's guitar playing looked so real. He was playing the notes even though the audience couldn't hear him and he was good enough to earn a compliment or two from musician Huey Lewis.

But Michael's early interest in rock faded when he discovered acting. Michael's initial reason for taking a drama class in high school is one many kids will understand. He joined to meet girls. But he soon developed an interest in acting for its own sake. When he was fifteen, a drama teacher told him that the Canadian Broadcasting Company was looking for an actor to play a ten-year-old in a series called "Leo and Me." Michael decided to audition. Because he was slim, and looked very young, he got the part. He appeared in a play called *The Shadow Box,* which proved a big hit in Vancouver, and was also cast in *Letters From Frank,* an American TV movie of the week filmed in Canada. The show starred Art Carney, Maureen Stapleton, and Margaret Hamilton, three highly skilled, vitally important performers. Michael found working with them very exciting.

Michael's parents wanted him to finish high school, but he quit school in his junior year. He had become totally involved in acting. When he was eighteen, he moved to Los Angeles. For a while things went well. He appeared on television in "Trapper John, M.D.," "Lou Grant," and Norman Lear's "Palmertown, U.S.A.," a series that lasted only a brief time. After that came the crash.

Acting isn't an easy profession and it's certainly not secure. Sometimes it just happens that an actor finds himself unemployed. His phone stops ringing. Auditions turn sour. Work dries up. It happened to Michael when he was twenty. He soon found himself in debt with no jobs in sight.

Michael J. Fox's hard-luck stories have become a Hollywood legend. Tales are told about how he lost twenty pounds living on a diet of macaroni, which was all he could afford to buy, how he supported himself selling his couch off section by section, and how he hung around a phone booth next to a Pioneer Chicken store when his phone was disconnected because he couldn't pay the bill. It was in that very phone booth that his agent told him about a role in an ongoing television series to be called "Family Ties." While they discussed the role with its weekly salary running in the thousands, all Michael could think of was how he wished he had a couple of dollars so he could go into the chicken store and buy something to eat.

But those rough days weren't all bad. He proved to himself and others that he was a tough survivor who was serious about his career. He would need that strength. The role of Alex Keaton didn't fall neatly into his lap. At first, the producer of "Family Ties" wasn't sure Michael should play the conservative preppie Alex. But Michael had the casting director on his side, and a second reading convinced the producer that Michael was right for the role.

Because "Family Ties" is such a successful sitcom, second in popularity only to "The Cosby Show," you may think it was a hit from the start. It wasn't. In the beginning, its ratings were low. "Family Ties" started out as a show about sixties-type liberal parents with conservative kids, but over the years this aspect softened and the characters changed. Michael did more than anyone else to make the show a hit, turning Alex into a character who is both charming and interesting. But developing a character takes time. At first Michael was scared of doing a television show before a live audience, and in the early episodes even the president of NBC wondered if Michael had been miscast.

But Michael got over his fears and devoted his boundless energy to bringing Alex to life. He succeeded so well, Alex is now the central character of the series and it would be hard to find anybody at NBC who has any complaints about Michael's performance. As the show's popularity grew, it brought Michael more work. Between seasons he'd appear as a guest on other TV shows. He did a telethon in Florida.

Michael J. Fox

Before *Back to the Future* gave Michael J. Fox his superstar status, he lived in a simple apartment in Bel Air, drove a Honda, and spent as much time as he could with his girlfriend, actress Nancy McKeon of the television series "The Facts of Life." They have since broken up. Today Michael lives in a three-bedroom ranch house with a pool in Laurel Canyon and drives a sleek Nissan 300ZX Turbo. But his work load isn't any lighter. If anything, he has even less time to relax and have fun.

Recreation for Michael consists mainly of reading Stephen King novels, going to movies and hockey games, listening to music, and playing racquetball. One of his best friends is rock star Julian Lennon. (Michael had a bit part in a Lennon video.) But Michael knows plenty of people who aren't stars. Some of his friends work on the Canadian railroad. They're guys he grew up with. Not long ago he zipped off to the famous Venice Film Festival with one of these old friends in tow.

Despite his busy schedule, Michael always snatches time somehow to work for charities. Because his nephew was born with the terrible disease spina bifida, the Spina Bifida Association is the charitable organization that has absorbed most of his time and energy. He is the association's national chairman of public awareness.

In the summer of 1985, "Family Ties" filmed a two-hour special in Britain. The idea of being in Britain was very exciting to Michael, but discipline is the key word in his vocabulary. There was little time to sightsee and practically no time for parties. He was up at seven every morning, working a sixteen-hour day. Though he made a splash reading for a role in *Pretty in Pink,* which starred Molly Ringwald, he was too busy making the "Family Ties" special to appear in the movie. The role went to Jon Cryer instead. Although Michael likes making movies, television means a lot to him. He enjoys playing Alex and will continue to appear on "Family Ties" for at least two to three more years.

The story of *Back to the Future* began for Michael when he was spotted by the film's producer, Stephen Spielberg. But once again Michael was too busy with "Family Ties" even to audition. Actually, Michael didn't even know he was being considered for the role of Marty. Nobody would tell him because everybody knew how disappointed he would be that he couldn't try out for the part. The role of Marty was given to Eric Stoltz, the talented young actor who played Rocky Dennis in *Mask*.

Five weeks into the shooting of the film, director Robert Zemeckis decided that Stoltz just wasn't right for Marty. Though recasting and

Michael J. Fox

reshooting would add three million dollars to the original fourteen-million-dollar film budget, both the producer and the director felt that they had no choice. With only a brief span of time left before "Family Ties" would be wrapped up and ready for its third season, Michael J. Fox was allowed to audition for Marty. He got the role. It turned out to be the biggest break of Michael's career.

Seven grueling weeks followed. Every day from 10:00 A.M. until 6:00 P.M., Michael was part of the hard-working team on "Family Ties." From 10:00 P.M. till at least 2:00 A.M., Michael worked feverishly on *Back to the Future*. He got to the point where he slept in sweat pants and a T-shirt so that he'd be ready the instant his alarm went off. Alex and Marty didn't suffer, but Michael was exhausted.

It was worth it. If *Back to the Future* did a lot for Michael J. Fox, he, in turn, did a lot for *Back to the Future*. Who can say whether the movie would have been such a spectacular hit if Michael hadn't been there to bring his special gifts to the film?

Back to the Future is a fantasy and comedy with a touch of "The Twilight Zone" about it. The hero, Marty McFly, is whisked back to 1955 in a time machine which takes the form of a De Lorean automobile. The time machine is the invention of a strange but appealing inventor played by Christopher Lloyd. Back in 1955, Marty accidentally makes a mess out of his parents' budding romance. He must find a way to bring them together or he, Marty, will cease to exist. Marty solves everything and winds up back in 1985 to discover that his parents, who were losers when he left, are now winners. The movie is an exciting adventure right until the very end.

The movie wouldn't click if Marty were a nerd or a genius. He must be a nice ordinary teenager so the audience will like him and believe in him. Michael J. Fox is the kind of actor who reminds most people of someone they know and like. He's also blessed with a great sense of comic timing. When it comes to television or movies, Michael has the audience on his side.

As far as Michael J. Fox is concerned, one of the best things about being a superstar is that people send him scripts. He doesn't have to audition. Thanks to receiving scripts, two new movies loom on the horizon and more will follow. *Light of Day* casts Michael as a young factory worker who plays the guitar. A change of pace for him, it's a serious drama set in the Cleveland, Ohio, area. Rock superstar Bruce Springsteen has written some of the movie's music and rock musician Joan Jett makes her screen debut in the film. Michael's also doing a

Michael J. Fox

romantic comedy. In addition, the sequel to *Back to the Future* may be shot this year.

People keep comparing Michael to James Cagney, an actor admired by millions of fans, who is best remembered for his movies of the 1930s, '40s, and '50s. Michael may even appear in a CBS-TV movie about James Cagney's early career. So, remember, if anyone asks you who's the hottest young star around, just answer Michael J. Fox. Most people will agree with you.

ALLY SHEEDY

On a winter day in 1982, a casting agent scooped up a picture of an unknown young actress named Ally Sheedy and liked what she saw. The casting agent was trying to find just the right actress to appear with Sean Penn in an upcoming movie called *Bad Boys*. Though Ally was twenty, she looked younger, and though she was pretty, she wasn't ultra-glamorous or ultra-gorgeous. That was just fine with the casting agent. She was looking for a girl audiences would find believable.

When the casting agent was quite sure that of the dozens upon dozens of actresses eager to appear in *Bad Boys*, Ally Sheedy was the best choice, she talked the movie's director Rick Rosenthal into giving Ally a chance. Ally got the role. After *Bad Boys*, Ally was in a string of

Ally Sheedy
(Courtesy PMK)

popular movies beginning with *War Games*, starring Matthew Broderick. Next came *Oxford Blues* with Rob Lowe. Then for a change of pace, Ally played the weird girl in *The Breakfast Club* with Anthony Michael Hall, Molly Ringwald, and other up-and-coming young stars. The star-studded *St. Elmo's Fire* followed. Ally was a young bride in *Twice in a Lifetime,* then went on to make *Blue City* with Judd Nelson. Teens so loved watching Ally make friends with a robot in *Short Circuit* that the movie was a smash hit.

Making successful film after successful film just seems to come naturally to Ally Sheedy. Audiences can't get enough of the slender five-foot-seven ex-ballet dancer with the gold-flecked eyes and broad, engaging grin. Acting was sort of a second career for Ally. She had already written a best-selling book for children when she was only twelve!

She was born on June 13, 1962, in New York City. In a lot of ways Ally Sheedy was a very lucky kid. Her father is a successful advertising executive. Her mother, Charlotte Sheedy, is a well-known literary agent who manages the careers of more than two hundred authors. With such high achievers for parents, it's no wonder that Ally is a high achiever, too. It runs in the family. Ally has a brainy younger brother and a younger sister who attends Skidmore College

Ally Sheedy

and plans to become a doctor. Ally herself was a dancer with the prestigious American Ballet Theater by the early age of seven. She also studied acting at New York's famous Neighborhood Playhouse, took art lessons, and went to some of New York's fanciest private schools including L'Ecole Français, the Bank Street School, and Columbia Prep.

Despite the advantages, Ally Sheedy was no spoiled rich kid. Part of the reason for all the lessons was that after her parents' divorce when she was nine, her parents were so busy with their separate careers that they had to find some way to keep their kids busy, too. So lessons kept the children safe and happily occupied during business hours. Ally's parents had apartments in the same Manhattan neighborhood and the Sheedy children never had to choose which parent to live with. They lived with both by moving back and forth between the two apartments. Of course, sometimes things got pretty confusing. Ally could never remember which apartment she'd left her sneakers in and her friends could never figure out whether they should call her at her father's or mother's.

Among Ally's many talents was a flair for writing, and in her early teens she described the anger and hurt she felt over her parents' divorce in a section of an article called "Mothers and Daughters" which appeared in *MS* magazine. She went on to write articles about movies for *The New York Times* and had works published in *The Village Voice,* two of New York's most important publications. But then Ally was forever making up stories. When she was nine and her mother went back to college, Ally would wander around the Columbia University campus thinking up dreamy tales. Leprechauns, elves, and mermaids filled her imagination.

Not surprisingly, she loved to read as well as write. When she was quite small, she memorized every word of the film *The Wizard of Oz* and acted out the roles of all the characters from Dorothy to the Scarecrow to the Wicked Witch and the Cowardly Lion. She also saw a movie called *Anne of the Thousand Days* when she was a child. The movie told the story of England's King Henry VIII and his second wife, Anne Boleyn. The movie's historical setting and lavish costumes stirred Ally Sheedy's love of drama. She began reading history books about the English kings and queens of old, especially Henry VIII's daughter Queen Elizabeth I.

At age twelve, Ally actually wrote a novel for young children about a London mouse who inherits the diary of a mouse who lived during the reign of Queen Elizabeth I. The book is

Ally Sheedy

called *She Was Nice to Mice*. Ally's mother helped her sell the book to a major publisher. It was so charming it became a best-seller, and Ally appeared with her mother on television's "Phil Donahue" show. She then appeared on her own on another TV talk show, "The Mike Douglas Show." While talking about her book and her interest in writing, she admitted that what she really wanted was to become an actress. When she got home she received a phone call from an agent whose job is to oversee the careers of actors and actresses. The agent had caught the show, thought Ally showed promise, and offered to manage her career.

But Charlotte Sheedy was no stage mother. She had high hopes for her daughter to become a writer. She allowed Ally to pursue an acting career provided acting didn't change Ally for the worse. She warned her daughter that if she became the kind of girl who spent all her time staring in the mirror, there would be no more acting. Ally's mother's high ideals and strong values stem from her days as a leader in the women's liberation movement and the peace movement of the 1960s and 1970s. One day when Ally was eight years old she answered the phone to learn that her mother was calling her from jail! Charlotte Sheedy had been arrested at an anti-war demonstration. She told Ally not to worry and promised she would be back home the next day, and she was.

Ally weathered a stint of acting in commercials without becoming the least bit conceited. But then success never affected Ally that way. Take her writing. Ally was in seventh grade when her novel was published. Overwhelmed by the attention it brought her, she tried to pretend to her friends that she hadn't written the book. Writing became so scary, she could barely bring herself to finish the themes and essays her teachers assigned her.

Once she began acting, Ally Sheedy realized that it was definitely the right career for her and in the end her mother allowed her to make her own independent decision. As for Ally's father, he was wildly proud of her for choosing acting and making a success of it. When he first saw Ally in a movie, he announced to the whole audience that the girl on the screen was his daughter. After the movie was over, he phoned Ally to tell her how grown-up she looked, but how even so, he kept remembering her as a baby. It was a sweet thing to say and it made Ally happy.

Besides commercials, Ally's acting career in high school included parts in off-Broadway plays. But she was drawn to movies and when she was seventeen, she flew to Los Angeles. It was a tough move. Ally cried all the way to the airport, asking herself if she wasn't making a big mistake. She didn't know anyone in Los Angeles. Living in the midst of buses and subways all her life, she didn't even know how to drive. How would she get around in a city where a car is a basic necessity?

But as soon as Ally arrived in California she felt better. The idea of not knowing anyone began to seem exciting. Making friends would be a challenge. She moved into an apartment, got a pet bird, and found a job as a waitress at a health food restaurant called Nature's Health Cove in Westwood. Ally, who thrives on health foods, has been a vegetarian since she turned thirteen.

Though Ally's rise to the top was quick, she had her share of ups and downs at first, like most young performers. In addition to working as a waitress, she made money doing commercials. Ally has appeared in a number of commercials advertising popular products, including Clearasil, McDonald's hamburgers, and Pizza Hut pizzas. But there were times when she couldn't find any work at all and had to borrow enough to live on from her father.

Eventually she landed a role in an ABC afterschool television special and appeared in bit roles in movies. Appearing in movies, even in small roles, gave her a chance to work with more experienced actresses like Melissa

Gilbert and Jennifer Jason Leigh. She played Jo in a radio version of *Little Women*. Julie Harris, a great actress known mainly for her work in live theater, was in the cast with Ally, and Ally learned a great deal about self-discipline from her.

But despite these useful experiences, there were disappointments. Ally was up for a lead in a television series called "Paper Dolls" and when she didn't get it, she was crushed. But the series failed anyway and a guest spot on "Hill Street Blues" gave her career a boost. Then came her big break in *Bad Boys* and soon she was more than a co-star—she was a major movie star.

What is Ally Sheedy like today? True to family tradition, she's a feminist with a strong social conscience. The bumper sticker on Ally's black Jeep reads "Visualize World Peace." She donates money to organizations that help abused children and battered women. She also makes donations to charities that fight hunger. One of her favorite causes is the protection of endangered species. Ally helps raise funds for political candidates who share her ideas.

Ally used to love to take long walks along Manhattan's streets, but now that she lives in a house near the beach in the Pacific Palisades, she takes long walks along the beach instead.

Ally Sheedy

She likes to shop for things for her house and even enjoys cleaning her home and taking care of it. Unlike many actresses who tend to know only people who work in the film industry, Ally has a lot of friends outside show business. Still, she counts movie star Rebecca De Mornay among her close friends. Ally's present boyfriend is a guitar player named Steve, best described as a really nice guy. Ally isn't attracted to macho-type males. Thoughtfulness means a lot to her and she values her independence.

As if making movies wasn't enough to keep her busy, Ally is a student at the University of Southern California. She's studying both anthropology and acting. This might be a heavy load for most people, but not for Ally Sheedy, whose house is crammed with books. The little girl who loved to read has grown up into a woman who loves to read.

Being Ally, she doesn't stop at reading. She's filled diaries and notebooks with stories and poems. A half-finished novel lies buried in a drawer. Ally hopes to complete it someday, but she believes she should wait until she's older and can bring a higher level of experience and maturity to her writing. Ally takes writing so seriously, she's considered having any future book published under a different name. She doesn't want to cash in on being Ally Sheedy, famous actress. Instead, she'd like people to discover her books for themselves and, of course, she hopes readers will like them.

But whether Ally Sheedy becomes a writer or an anthropologist someday, in the here and now what she loves most is acting. She even loves auditioning for roles. That's because she believes it's good to try new things and take risks. She admits that it hurts when you don't get the role you want, and that happens often, even to stars.

Whatever roles Ally's missed, she's certainly landed plenty of good ones. Ally Sheedy fans can usually find their heroine right up on the screen of a nearby movie theater. It's a long way from Manhattan to Los Angeles, but Ally Sheedy has made the trip in style.

TOM CRUISE

Conventional wisdom holds that if you're going to make it big in films while you are still young, you need to come from a family with either a lot of money or one that is in show business or has show business connections.

Thomas Cruise Mapother IV shortened his name and skipped his high school graduation in order to hit the streets of New York to try to make it as an actor. His previous experience—playing Nathan Detroit in his high school production of *Guys and Dolls.*

By the time he was twenty-one, he was the star of *Risky Business,* not only a film but *the* film of the MTV generation. His *Top Gun* was the biggest hit of the summer of '86. *The Color of Money,* with Paul Newman, was the top hit of the fall of '86. He is an established superstar who commands well over $1 million a picture. He's not just a hyped-up model, either. Tom Cruise can act and his future seems assured.

So much for conventional wisdom.

Tom Cruise was born in Syracuse, New York, on July 3, 1962, the third of four children. His father was an electrical engineer and sometime inventor who moved around a lot. While Tom was growing up, he lived in half a dozen different towns in the U.S. and Canada.

Tom's mother, Mary Lee, had always been interested in acting. Wherever the family moved, she became involved in some kind of local theater group. When the family settled in Ottawa, Canada, she even helped form an amateur group. But Mary Lee had never really thought of acting professionally. She said that when she was growing up, the idea of going to Hollywood seemed completely out of the question for nice girls.

Mary Lee says that Tom liked to do imitations and little skits when he was a small child, but that phase didn't last long. As soon as he got older, all his energy went into sports. According to his mother, sports gave him a chance to excel and to make friends. Tom suffered from a learning disability called dyslexia, which makes reading difficult. Classroom work was sometimes an agony for him and teachers didn't

Tom Cruise
(Retna Ltd.)

always understand. In addition moving around a lot made it tough to establish friendships.

The biggest trauma in Tom's life came when he was twelve. His parents divorced. For a boy who had moved around all his life and had no real roots in any community, this family breakup came as an unusually severe blow.

Tom's mother took the family back to her native Louisville, Kentucky. Money was scarce, and life was hard. Mary Lee worked at a variety of jobs, just to keep the family together. The kids pitched in doing what work they could. Tom had a paper route.

School didn't get any easier for him and Tom felt that he never fitted in. He told a reporter for *Rolling Stone* magazine, "I look back upon high school and grade school and I would never want to go back there. Not in a million years." All he wanted to do was "get through it."

Life improved a lot after Mary Lee remarried. Tom recalls feeling threatened at first, but after a while he came to both respect and love his stepfather. The family moved to Glen Ridge, New Jersey, where Tom finished high school.

Still, Tom didn't know what he was going to do with his life. While he participated in lots of sports, he was not really a great athlete. He was just intense, and tried to make up in energy what he lacked in skill. He was best at wrestling, and there was a possibility that he might get a wrestling scholarship to some college. But then he was injured, and that ended that. He thought about traveling for a few years before trying college.

It was about this time that his glee club instructor told him to try out for the school musical—which happened to be *Guys and Dolls*. He got the lead. Suddenly his whole life turned around. Tom found that he loved performing. Nothing that he had ever experienced before matched the thrill of being on stage. For the first time he had a focus for his life.

After the show, he sat down and had a serious talk with his mother and stepfather. He told them he wanted to try to go into show business. He said that he wanted ten years to give it a try. His stepfather had some reservations. "Ten years," he thought. "How much is this going to cost?" But both Mary Lee and her husband had simply been bowled over by Tom's performance. They felt he had real talent, and if show business was what he wanted to do, then he should give it his best shot. They may have been nervous, they may have had reservations, but they both gave him their blessing.

Eighteen-year-old Tom Cruise hit the streets of New York City. Like thousands of other aspiring young actors, he waited on tables during the evenings so that he could go to auditions during the day. He picked up acting classes and workshop productions when he could. He also appeared in a dinner theater production of *Godspell.*

But unlike those thousands of other young actors, Tom Cruise didn't have to wait for years to be noticed. He's handsome, but so are lots of other young actors. On stage he displayed an intensity that was absolutely riveting. He was the sort of actor who had to be noticed. And noticed he was. Within five months he had been given a small part in the Brooke Shields film *Endless Love.* That film may have done more for Tom's career than it did for Brook's.

A few months later he got another small part in *Taps,* a film about a group of cadets who take over a military academy. The stars of the film were a pair of hot young actors, Timothy Hutton and Sean Penn. Also appearing was the great veteran actor George C. Scott. Tom had originally been cast in a very minor role, but he was so intense, so sincere, that he was offered a much better role—that of the hotheaded cadet David Shawn.

His next film, *Losin' It,* released in 1983, was a bit of an embarrassment. It was quite frankly a teen exploitation film, about a bunch of kids going down to Tijuana, Mexico, for the first time. Tom learned something from that film, bad as it may have been. Before *Losin' It,* he was under the impression that all you had to do

Tom Cruise

to make a great film was to work really hard. He worked hard on *Losin' It* and it still wasn't a good film. He learned that if you want to build a successful film career you have to be very careful about the movies in which you choose to appear.

Tom made it clear that he wanted to develop his skills as an actor. He wasn't interested in just making money. He wanted to appear in the best films that he possibly could, and work with the best people.

In his next film, *The Outsiders,* he met one of the best, director Francis Ford Coppola, who had directed *The Godfather.* But it was the film after that, *Risky Business,* that provided the big breakthrough for Tom's career.

The scene in which Joel Goodsen (Tom Cruise), wearing only a button-down shirt and underwear, struts around playing an imaginary guitar to Bob Seger's "Old Time Rock & Roll" is one of the truly memorable sequences in modern film history. It's been imitated and parodied endlessly. Everyone knows it.

Risky Business was a box office blockbuster. A relatively low-budget film, it made $65 million in movie theaters alone. And that doesn't count the money from cable TV and videocassette rentals.

In *Risky Business* Tom Cruise was a rich kid headed for Princeton. In his next film, *All the*

Right Moves, he was a poor kid, living in a decaying small town in the middle of the rust belt. His only chance to go to college was to win a football scholarship. *All the Right Moves* wasn't the blockbuster that *Risky Business* had been, but it got generally good reviews, and Cruise turned in a solid and believable performance.

Tom Cruise wanted to become an actor. *Risky Business* made him something more—it made him a star, and it made him a celebrity. When he started dating his *Risky Business* costar Rebecca De Mornay, the gossip columnists couldn't get enough of him. Photographers started following him around. A lot of young actors, when they are suddenly catapulted to stardom, let their egos run away with them. They become puffed with self importance and impossible to deal with. This hasn't happened to Tom. Most of those who work with him have found him remarkably kind and very natural.

With the success of *Risky Business* behind him, Tom could command a reported $1 million per picture. A few other stars get more, but for a twenty-one-year-old, who seemed to have come out of nowhere, this was enormous success. It put Tom Cruise in the front rank of Hollywood stars. It also gave him an opportunity to really take control of his own career. He had his pick of projects.

Tom Cruise

Cruise said he wanted to work with the best, so he next decided to work with director Ridley Scott. Scott is one of the best directors of imaginative films working today. He directed the films *Alien* and *Blade Runner*—two science fiction classics. The project was *Legend,* an elaborate fairy tale in which Cruise played Jack o' the Green, an agent of goodness. It looked like a bold and imaginative career move for Tom. But sometimes bold and imaginative moves don't work out as planned.

Legend, which was filmed in London, seemed to be jinxed right from the start. There were all sorts of production problems. Then right in the middle of the filming, the whole set burned down. *Legend* took more than a year to film. Tom was isolated in London. His romance with De Mornay broke up. When *Legend* was finally released it bombed—badly. No one, not the audience, not the critics, not Tom Cruise was satisfied. "I'll never want to do another picture like that again," said Tom.

No good actor's career ever runs smoothly uphill. There are always going to be failures along the way. The actor who doesn't take any chances, who keeps making the same type of movie over and over again, will never grow.

Tom needed a new project to get his career back on track. The project was already looking for him. A couple of producers were interested in doing a film about the training of elite fighter pilots. From the start, the producers had Tom Cruise in mind for the lead. He was still in London working on the long-delayed *Legend*. So they waited.

When Cruise finished *Legend,* he was very cautious about taking on new pictures. He wanted to make sure they would work for him before he committed himself. He asked the producers if he could take a couple of months and help write the script before he would agree to do the film. It was a very unusual deal, but the producers wanted Tom Cruise very badly, so they agreed. After two months Cruise decided that this was indeed his kind of film.

The film was, of course, *Top Gun,* the biggest hit of the summer of '86.

Tom Cruise fans will argue whether he was better as Joel Goodsen in *Risky Business,* or Pete "Maverick" Mitchell in *Top Gun*. It's not much of an argument. He was terrific as both.

Tom's next film project is *The Color of Money,* which was shot in Chicago early in 1986. He had not abandoned his plan to work with the best. The director of the film is Martin Scorsese, acknowledged to be one of the most creative film directors working today. His co-star is film legend Paul Newman. The film itself is sort of a sequel to the 1961 Newman classic, *The Hustler.* The ambitious but flaky young pool hustler, Vincent Lauria, is yet another in Cruise's gallery of memorable characters.

When Tom told his mother and stepfather that he wanted to try and become an actor, he said he wanted to give himself ten years to see if he could make it. It hasn't been quite ten years yet, but I think that we can definitely say that he has made it.

DEMI MOORE

When Demi Moore finally decided to become an actress, she enrolled in an acting class. The class terrified her. She was constantly afraid that she would be called on to get up and do a scene. So she started skipping class. What did she do with her free time? She went out and got acting jobs. "Somehow, it was a lot easier for me to go out and try to get the jobs," she told *Elle* magazine.

But then Demi Moore has always had to make it on her own. Unlike a lot of today's young stars, Demi started with *no* advantages. She was born Demi Guynes on November 11, 1963, in Roswell, New Mexico. Her parents, Danny and Virginia Guynes, were practically teenagers themselves. Her father had a job that required lots of moving and it seemed to Demi

Demi Moore
(Retna Ltd.)

that she had a new home every six months. Every time she had to move, she had to adjust to a new house, a new neighborhood, a new school. It was tough because she felt that she had no real place in the world, and no real sense of who she was. All she wanted to do was "be okay and belong."

Her parents separated while she was a teenager. Demi, with no sense of security, and tired of the sort of life she had been leading, dropped out of school when she was only sixteen. At that point she felt that she had to take control of her own life. She recalls that her mother accepted the decision without any argument.

Demi and her mother had been living in Los Angeles at the time, and she quickly picked up a job as a receptionist in a collection agency. A few years later she married British songwriter and musician Freddy Moore. Although they soon divorced, she did keep the name.

Demi had ambitions that went well beyond answering phones. Pretty, slightly wistful, with a flawless complexion and large dark eyes, Demi had no problem getting modeling jobs. But that was only a means to an end, and the end was becoming an actress. That's when she started taking those acting lessons that she found so intimidating. The acting jobs came more easily. First, there were small parts in films like *Young Doctors in Love* and *Choices*.

Demi Moore

Her big break came when she was only nineteen. She snared the coveted role of Jackie Templeton on TV's hit soap, "General Hospital." Her TV "medical career" lasted for two years, and before it was over she was a minor celebrity. People on the street recognized her, and would stop and stare. Some would come up and ask her silly questions just to hear her speak.

The voice—that's probably Demi's most distinctive feature. There are lots of pretty young girls in Hollywood, but she is, according to *Time* magazine, "The One with the Voice, a rough, sexy rumble that can loosen a male viewer's necktie." The worldly voice contrasts starkly with the innocent face, making Demi's presence memorable.

Demi's sort of fame, however, does not automatically bring good roles. She had a part in the 3-D shocker, *Parasite,* a movie which proved to be a horror film in more ways than one. Then there was a chance to play opposite the veteran actor Michael Caine in a film called *Blame it on Rio.* It looked like a big opportunity, but the film turned out to be a real bomb.

St. Elmo's Fire may have done more for Demi's career than it did for the careers of its other young stars. She really stood out from the crowd as Jules, the spoiled, troubled rich girl. Her performance was solid, believable, and compelling. And of course there was The Voice. She was even better in *No Small Affair*, as the warm-hearted pop singer pursued by the nerdy teenage photographer played by Jon Cryer. She teamed up with Rob Lowe for the popular '86 film, *About Last Night*, and at this writing is awaiting the release of *Wisdom*, in which she costars with fiancé Emilio Estevez. She also did an off-Broadway show, *The Early Girl*, in the fall of '86.

Looking back on her life so far, Demi cannot say that it has always been easy or pleasant. There have been frantic periods with "a lot of late nights."

But right now she's taking her career very seriously, and that means that she has to take very good care of herself. Demi has become a nonsmoking, nondrinking vegetarian who exercises rigorously every day. Though she never finished high school, she has plunged into reading authors like Dostoyevski.

Recently she told writer Vanda Krefft, "I can't say that I've lived a life without pain. But everthing in my life contributes to why I am where I am. And I'm really happy. I can say today, I'm really a happy person."

Like all young actors and actresses, twenty-four-year-old Demi Moore faces some major career decisions. She is no longer a teenage actress, and unlike some, she doesn't look like a teenager anymore. She must now make the transition to fully adult roles. It's a tricky period in any career, and lots don't make it. We're betting that "The One with the Voice" does.

ROB LOWE

It sometimes seems to Rob Lowe that he was born under a lucky star. As far back as he can remember, he has had one burning ambition in life—to become a successful actor. Not only has he achieved that goal, but at the age of twenty-two, he's moved beyond acting into writing and producing. This triple achievement makes him a triple success. But then three may be Rob's lucky number. He's been blessed with a trio of natural gifts. First, there's his looks. Most girls would agree that Rob Lowe is the most handsome movie star around. But you don't become a successful actor on looks alone. Rob's got charm and talent as well.

Born in Dayton, Ohio, Rob began his career acting in summer stock, making commercials, and appearing on local television. California,

Rob Lowe
(Courtesy PMK)

home of the film industry, beckoned and Rob moved with his family to Santa Monica. It was at Santa Monica High School that Rob met a young actor named Emilio Estevez. They would meet again later on screen.

In California Rob continued where he'd left off in Ohio. He made some more commercials and appeared on television. Only this time it wasn't local television. Rob landed parts in two ABC television After School Specials. He was in "Schoolboy Father" and had a role in "A Matter of Time," which won an Emmy Award. Next came two series pilots, "Mean Jeans" and "Thrills and Chills." He then appeared on the ABC series "A New Kind of Family."

Movies entered Rob Lowe's life when he made his film debut in *The Outsiders,* which was based on a novel by S. E. Hinton. The 1982 movie was directed by Francis Ford Coppola, and Rob played a character named Sodapop. Rob's career moved a giant step forward when he was given a role in the 1983 television movie *Thursday's Child,* which starred the highly respected actress Gina Rowlands. Rob's performance as a teenager in need of a heart transplant won him a Golden Globe Award nomination.

Next came the film *Class* with Rob cast as Jacqueline Bisset's prep school son. He went on to appear in *The Hotel New Hampshire,* a movie based on the novel by John Irving. Rob shot to stardom in *Oxford Blues* with Ally Sheedy. His star rose even higher when teenagers flocked to see the 1985 movie *St. Elmo's Fire,* which featured a glittering cast of young actors and actresses. The film told the story of a group of Georgetown University graduates trying to adjust to life after college. Several critics dubbed the movie "the little chill" because its theme reminded them of another popular movie called *The Big Chill.* One difference between the two movies is the age of the actors. *The Big Chill* concerns an older group. In *St. Elmo's Fire* Rob plays saxophone player Billy Hixx, who runs away from his problems by trying to relive his college days.

Rob took a break from his busy film schedule to appear in a music video you may have seen called *Turn to You* made by the Go-Go's, an all-woman rock band which has since split up. The winter of 1985–86 saw the debut of Rob's movie *Youngblood* in which he portrayed an American hockey player getting started in professional sports. Then, at his agent's urging, he broke a dinner date to stay home and read a script. It turned out to be the script for a comedy called *About Last Night*. Rob liked the script so much, he jumped at the chance to make the film.

In the movie he plays a restaurant supply salesman named Danny who falls in love with

Rob Lowe and longtime girlfriend Melissa Gilbert
(Walter McBride/Retna Ltd.)

Debbie Sullivan, played by Demi Moore. But despite his feelings, the handsome Rob is unwilling to settle down. Only when he is about to lose Demi does he realize how much he loves her. Co-starring with Rob and Demi are Elizabeth Perkins and Jim Belushi.

As of this writing, there are two more films on Rob's agenda. The first is *Square Dance,* to be shot in the Dallas, Texas, area. In *Square Dance,* directed by Daniel Petrie, Rob plays a retarded young man. Co-starring with Rob are two of America's most highly acclaimed performers, actor Jason Robards and actress Jane Alexander. Debi Richter of "Hill Street Blues" and Winona Ryder, who was in *Lucas,* are also in the film. One of the producers of *Square Dance* is former Monkee Mike Nesmith.

Rob's other upcoming project is the movie that will launch his new production company. Called *Something Else,* the movie will tell the life story of fifties rockabilly star Eddie Cochran. It's to be shot in Eddie's home state of Oklahoma and in neighboring Texas. *Something Else* will also touch on the lives of two of Eddie's friends, music legends Buddy Holly and Gene Vincent. Rob will sing lots of the hit songs of the era, including Eddie Cochran's great classic, "Summertime Blues." In keeping with the spirit of *Square Dance* and *Something*

Else, Rob took time to appear at the Farm Aid benefit hosted by country singer Willy Nelson.

When Rob isn't working, he spends time with his long-term girlfriend, Melissa Gilbert, or with his nineteen-year-old brother, Chad, who is also an actor. Chad, too, has inherited the Lowe family's good looks. What are Rob's goals? Well, at this point in his life, his central concern is to keep learning about himself and to continue fulfilling that burning childhood ambition of succeeding as an actor. He's certainly carved a place for himself in Hollywood and started a promising career. No wonder Rob Lowe has named his production company Lucky Star.

LAURA DERN

Laura Dern tried out for a part in *The Breakfast Club,* but she didn't get it. The rejection didn't bother her that much. Of all today's young stars, Laura probably has the most easygoing attitude about Hollywood success.

That ease should come as no surprise because Laura knows Hollywood as well as anybody. Her father is the actor Bruce Dern, her mother, actress Diane Ladd. When she was growing up, Susan Strasberg and Shelley Winters were "like godmothers" to her. One of her father's closest friends was Jack Nicholson. You can't get more Hollywood than that.

Laura doesn't just come from Hollywood aristocracy, she also comes from American aristocracy. Her great-grandfather George Dern was Secretary of War under President Franklin

Delano Roosevelt. She is also related to the celebrated American poet Archibald MacLeish and playwright Tennessee Williams. She was in the social register, but declined the traditional debutante's coming-out party because she thought the ritual was "trivial."

Laura's parents were divorced when she was only two. Her mother traveled a great deal because of her acting career, and Laura spent a lot of time in the care of her maternal grandmother. Her grandmother, she says, was "incredibly imaginative." Thinking back on those years, she realizes that her grandmother's imagination was a major influence on her own development as an actress. She says that while you're playing a role you have to imagine you really are that person in order to be convincing.

Laura's mother remarried a New York stockbroker and moved to the Upper East Side of Manhattan. Laura never really adjusted to the city, and after her mother's second divorce, she happily moved right back to Santa Monica.

Laura made her first film at the age of seven. She was an extra in the film *Alice Doesn't Live Here Anymore*. Her mother had the role of Flo. Laura had to eat a banana ice cream cone in one scene. That seemed easy enough, but the scene had to be reshot nineteen times, not because of what Laura was doing, but because of the main action in the scene. When it was over she was throughly sick of banana ice cream. That's a part of screen acting that most people don't think about. Scenes have to be shot over and over again. Director Martin Scorsese was impressed. He figured that if she could eat that many ice cream cones, she had to be an actress.

Laura, however, did not jump directly into an acting career. She even started college, though she left after one semester. She didn't like the mandatory courses, and her film work was picking up.

By far her most important film to date is *Smooth Talk*. Although Laura plays a teenager in the film, it is not your typical Hollywood teen film. It is really more of what is called an "art film." *Smooth Talk* was a low-budget film with limited distribution. Naturally it wasn't a huge box office success, but critics and lots of serious film buffs loved it. They particularly loved Laura's Connie.

The way she got that role shows the importance of connections in Hollywood. Director Joyce Chopra had cast all the parts except that of Connie, the lead. She was looking around for an actress who could be a mature woman one moment, a young girl the next. Chopra was having a tough time finding someone to fill the part. Then a photographer who was working on the film mentioned Laura Dern. "She's the daughter of my neighbor Bruce Dern." Laura went in to read for the part. Connections definitely helped her get a foot in the door, but once the reading started, connections didn't count anymore. She was on her own. Director Chopra was not merely impressed, she was practically bowled over. So were the critics after the film opened.

Laura's next film, *Mask,* attracted a much wider audience. Laura wasn't the star. Most of the attention went to Cher and to Eric Stoltz, who played the horribly disfigured boy, Rocky. But Laura, as the blind girl who falls in love with Rocky, was both effective and affecting. Her reviews have been so good that Laura is a little nervous that her next picture will be a disappointment to her growing band of boosters and admirers.

The picture, *Blue Velvet,* is a strange and controversial thriller about an innocent girl who gets involved in a murder. Starring in it along with Laura are Isabella Rossellini and Laura's current boyfriend, Kyle MacLachlan. You may remember him, he was the star of *Dune.* On the other hand you may not remember him, because *Dune* was a multimillion dollar turkey that audiences stayed away from in droves. MacLachlan, however, had an impressive theatrical background before he was cast in *Dune.* Laura insists that *Blue Velvet* is

Laura Dern and Kyle MacLachlan
(Tammie Arroyo/Retna Ltd.)

not her movie and that the parts played by Rossellini and MacLachlan may be the ones the audience finds most interesting.

Laura Dern is attractive, but her beauty doesn't knock you over. *Time* magazine describes the blond five-foot-ten Laura as looking "as if she should be playing power forward on the UCLA women's basketball team." In interviews she comes across as very California, almost flakey California. She's into all sorts of offbeat things and believes in reincarnation, as well as handling rock crystals "to pick up energy." When filming *Mask,* which is based on the story of a real boy, she felt the "essence" of the real Rocky was on the set.

Though she loves California, there are a lot of things about Hollywood and the Hollywood life that she doesn't like at all. She doesn't like its arrogance, and its phoniness. Laura knows enough about Hollywood fame to realize that today's star can be tomorrow's case of "whatever happened to . . ."

The key, she believes, is not just who you hang around with, or who you are photographed with, but the quality of the work that you do. She's incredibly serious and hardworking. In preparing for the part of the blind girl in *Mask,* she wore a blindfold for ten days, just to get some idea of what blindness would feel like.

Laura Dern

There is nothing flakey about Laura's work habits.

Laura Dern has loads of ideas about what she would like to do with her career. But one thing she would *love* to do is a Woody Allen movie. She has good taste.

RALPH MACCHIO

"I don't want to be the Sylvester Stallone of Karate Kid movies." That's what Ralph Macchio said when interviewed recently by *People* magazine. The reason for the interview was the stunning success of *Karate Kid II*. The success of the sequel not only surprised Macchio, it alarmed him a bit. "I'm not interested in making twelve sequels. If they come up with *Karate Kid III*, I'll certainly look at the script, but I want to try different characters."

And that's just exactly what he did. Right after *Karate Kid II*, Macchio went to Broadway, or to be more exact off-Broadway. He was to appear in a play with his own personal acting idol, Robert DeNiro. The play, *Cuba and His Teddy Bear*, was a tough, gritty, and distinctly

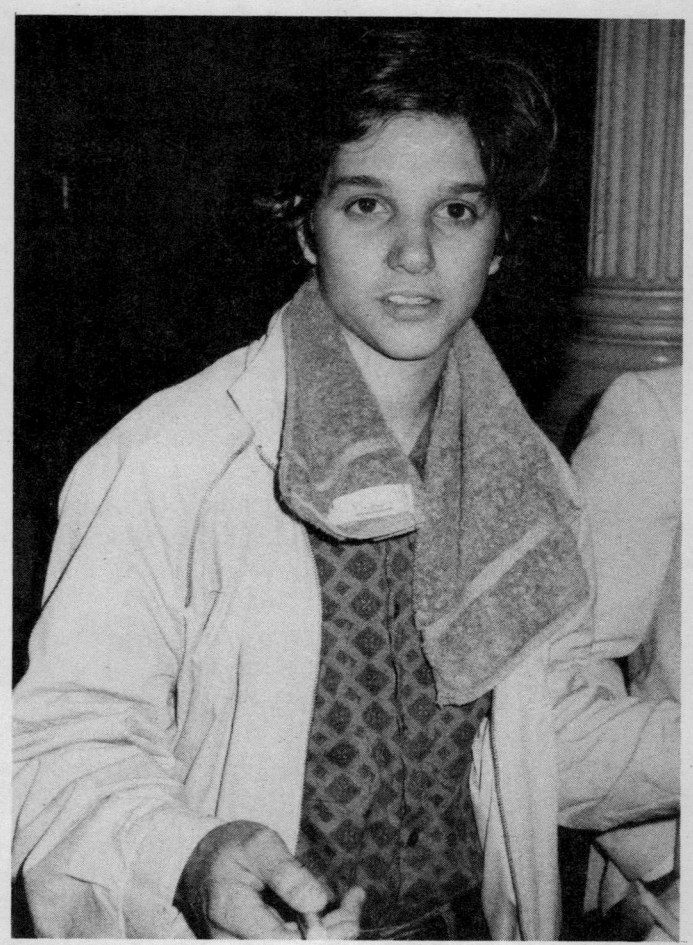

Ralph Macchio
(Walter McBride/Retna Ltd.)

downbeat show. It's not the sort of play that's turned into a movie blockbuster. Macchio played a Hispanic teenager (Teddy) who is both attracted and repelled by his half-crazed, drug dealer father (Cuba), played by DeNiro. When word got around that DeNiro and Macchio were to appear on stage together, tickets went like crazy. The entire limited run of the show was sold out. The stars were so hot that rehearsals had to be held in secret to keep the fans away. The man who engineered this theater coup was Joseph Papp, probably America's most innovative producer for the live theater.

Papp is always looking for new ways to attract young people to the theater. He figured putting a teen-screen idol like Ralph Macchio on stage would be a perfect way of doing that. And the gamble worked for him.

But appearing in *Cuba and His Teddy Bear* was a much bigger gamble for Ralph. It was what's known in the business as a "bold career move." Macchio had no real stage experience. He had to appear opposite one of the best actors in America. The play was not at all the sort that would appeal to the usual Karate Kid audience. The New York theater critics, who can be very mean, would all be out there watching him. A lot of screen actors have fallen on their faces trying to do live theater.

How did it work out? Not badly. The critics

noted Ralph's lack of stage experience, but they also said the kid has real talent.

Ralph loved working on stage. He loved the attention and energy he got from the live audience. And he loved working with DeNiro. "He's taught me that acting is limitless; you can go any place you want with it, any direction."

That's a big change for Ralph, who once expressed a "couldn't care less" attitude about acting.

Ralph was born on November 4, 1962. That's right, he's a lot older than he looks. Sometimes his youthful appearance bothers him. Even his younger brother Stephen looks older than he does. But the boyish appearance has done wonders for his career. He's been able to play a teenager a lot longer, and a lot more convincingly, than most young actors.

Ralph's hometown is Huntington, Long Island, where his family owns a trucking business. His mother signed him up for dancing lessons when he was only three, and he stuck with it. When he was sixteen he was spotted in a local dance recital by an agent who figured he could make some money in commercials. He did, but he wasn't all that impressed by doing commercials.

He was planning to go to C. W. Post college on Long Island when something bigger than a commercial came along. It was a part in the comedy *Up the Academy*. It wasn't a particularly good part, and the film wasn't very good either, but it was a start. Next, it was a season as Betty Buckley's adopted nephew in "Eight is Enough."

That was all lightweight stuff. When Ralph heard that Francis Ford Coppola, director of the *Godfather,* was casting for the film *The Outsiders,* Ralph went for it. He now admits that it was the first time in his career that he really cared about getting a part. And he got the part he wanted, a major role as teen rebel Johnny Cade. But somehow he wasn't satisfied with the film, or with his performance.

He wasn't satisfied with Hollywood either. He'd moved out there when he made his first film. After two years he moved back to Huntington. Ralph is close to his family, and "that Hollywood stuff can drive you crazy." He knows a lot of other actors, but his really close friends are the members of his family and some kids he's known since high school.

When Ralph was first shown the script for *The Karate Kid,* he wasn't exactly overwhelmed. He thought the film was going to be some sort of Bruce Lee parody. But after he read the script, he discovered it was more than that. *The Karate Kid* was really sort of a teenage *Rocky*. That's not surprising, because the

Ralph Macchio

film's director was John G. Avildsen, who won an Academy Award for directing *Rocky*.

The Karate Kid, as everyone knows, was an enormous popular success. The critics were less thrilled. But they did say that the chemistry between Ralph and Noriyuki "Pat" Morita, who plays the karate teacher and father figure, was terrific.

After *The Karate Kid* Ralph did *Teachers,* a sort of dark comedy starring Nick Nolte. Then he took on a TV film called *The Three Wishes of Billy Grier.* In it he plays a boy who has a disease called progeria. It's a disease that causes rapid aging. Ralph had to go from looking like he was a teenager to looking like he was ninety. That involved four-hour makeup sessions and painful applications of foam rubber and spirit gum. Despite all the pain, or perhaps because of it, Ralph still regards Billy Grier as one of his best performances.

For *The Karate Kid,* Ralph had to learn karate. For his next film, *Crossroads,* in which he played a professional guitar player, he had to learn to play the guitar. Before he took the part in *Crossroads,* he swears that he never even held a guitar before. *Crossroads* was not an enormous success, but Ralph's performance once again demonstrated that he was a lot more than the Karate Kid.

Young and Famous

You might think being a movie star is easy work. When Ralph was filming the original *Karate Kid,* he often worked twelve hours a day, seven days a week. In addition, he had to take karate lessons. *Crossroads* and *The Karate Kid II* were filmed back to back. That meant more twelve-hour days and seven-day weeks. And now, in addition to the karate practice, there were the guitar lessons. And right after that he went into rehearsals for *Cuba and His Teddy Bear.* And right after that he went into a case of pneumonia. Don't worry, he's fine now, but that kind of schedule does take its toll. It's a price that Ralph Macchio seems more than willing to pay for an acting career that he now takes very seriously indeed.

PHOEBE CATES

When she was ten, Phoebe Cates wanted to be a dancer. She even got a scholarship to the School of American Ballet. But then she received a serious knee injury. It didn't end her dancing career, but it did make her realize how dangerous and difficult dancing can be. "There's no life as a dancer, to me. It's a hard life and very few people succeed at it."

So she abandoned dancing and by the age of 15 she was launched on a career as a professional model. But that is also a career with a limited lifespan. So she decided to try acting.

Acting was not an unfamiliar life to Phoebe. Her father, Joseph Cates, is a long-time television producer. Her sister, Valerie, is an actress and her brother, Philip, is a director. But when she told her father that she wanted to try acting, he wasn't enthusiastic; in fact, "he kind of groaned." The actor's life is no easy one, either.

Her acting career to date has had some high points, and some lows. One of the lows was her first picture, *Paradise,* which she made when she was seventeen. Phoebe calls that a "learning experience." "What I learned was never to do a movie like that again." Another bomb was something called *Private School.*"

But there were high points. One was the extremely popular teen comedy *Fast Times at Ridgemont High,* which also starred Sean Penn. Phoebe remembers that film as the most fun to do, "because I was working with a bunch of people my own age. I made a lot of friends and got to do great improvisational work."

The real high point of her career, though, was the 1984 Stephen Spielberg hit *Gremlins.* It wasn't as much fun to film as *Ridgemont High,* since she was working with a lot of latex monsters rather than other young actors. Phoebe was fairly nervous on the set, and the crew knew it. They always had some sort of a surprise for her. She told reporter Peter Masley, "They would have a gremlin come up to you and tap you on the shoulder." There was a scene where they wouldn't tell her where a gremlin was going to pop up from. They finally had it come out of the hood of a car.

A lot of the screams that she let out in the

Phoebe Cates
(Courtesy APA)

movie were very realistic because they were very real. "They were pretty scary to look at," she said of the gremlins.

At one point during the filming she scared some other people, but not on purpose. Near the end of *Gremlins*, Phoebe and co-star Zach Galligan are supposed to have been injured by the creatures. They had their makeup and costumes on. She had a big bruise painted on her neck. His sweater was spattered with fake blood. The two of them were riding around the lot on a motor scooter when they hit something. Both were stunned but not really hurt. Near the scene of the accident was the set for the TV series "T.J. Hooker." "The guys . . . came running over, saw our wounds, and just freaked out."

Gremlins was, of course, a monster hit. In some quarters it was criticized as being too gruesome and violent, particularly for a kids' film, but Phoebe doesn't understand that sort of criticism. "Don't people watch cartoons? The Road Runner is always falling off a cliff and getting smashed."

Phoebe's next big role was a real change of pace. She played the wronged and embittered Lili in the enormously popular TV miniseries "Lace." The series was so popular that it was followed by "Lace II." No one, least of all Phoebe Cates, would claim that "Lace" was

Phoebe Cates
(Courtesy APA)

high art. Phoebe wasn't even particularly crazy about the character of Lili. "I couldn't relate to her," she says.

Phoebe has done more serious work on stage. In 1985 she appeared at Joseph Papp's Public Theater in New York. The play was *The Nest of the Wood Grouse,* a satire about life in Moscow today. A few months later she got the role of Nina, in a California production of the classic Russian play *The Sea Gull,* by Anton Chekhov.

She's also dating Kevin Kline, who, while he has appeared in films like *The Big Chill,* is widely regarded as one of America's leading stage actors.

Phoebe's stage success comes as something of a surprise to her. She once suffered from severe stage fright. "I used to panic when I had to read an essay before the class." She was still panicking when she began going on stage. "It became a matter of survival every night for me." Many actors suffer from stage fright at first. Most get over it eventually, though some famous actors suffer every time they appear in front of an audience. They just don't show it. Phoebe feels she has her fear under control, but not entirely beaten.

She has also done some singing, songwriting, and has recorded a couple of albums. But she doesn't want to sing in front of an audience. "I just want to be a studio artist. You can do some real neat things there, and I like getting involved in the whole sound. There's no way I'll ever perform."

ANTHONY MICHAEL HALL

Of today's young actors, Anthony Michael Hall is one of the most popular, and certainly one of the most accomplished.

Michael (that's what everybody calls him) was born in Boston, but now lives in New York with his mother, stepfather and younger stepsister. "My parents separated when I was very young. My mom struggled to raise me and pursue a career," says Michael. "It was very difficult for her but she did it. She is giving and gracious, but at the same time, she is creative and strong-willed."

Sometimes kids resent stepparents, but this has not been the case with Michael. "My stepfather and I adopted each other and I think of him as my dad. We're very close. He's calm and logical and good at assessing situations. I've

Anthony Michael Hall

learned a lot from him. Our family is close knit and we make decisions as a group." They are close, indeed, for Michael's stepfather is also his manager.

Michael attended the Professional Children's School in New York, a city he loves. Even today he stays in New York, rather than migrating to California, as many film actors have. Michael began acting at the age of eight, doing television commercials. His first major break came when comedian and talk show host Steve Allen cast him as the young Steve Allen in his semiautobiographical play, *The Wake*. It was the story of the day of his grandmother's funeral. "Working with someone of his [Allen's] caliber really turned me on to performing. It was very gratifying and it was something I felt I was good at," says Michael.

He then went into television and quickly amassed an impressive list of credits. He played the young Edgar Allen Poe in the Emmy Award-winning "Gold Bug." He was Huck Finn in "Rascals and Robbers." He also appeared in shows like "The Body Human" and "Running Out." His appearance on "Saturday Night Live" was a memorable one, both for the audience and for Michael.

He hasn't ignored the stage, appearing in such off-Broadway shows as *St. Joan of the Microphone* and *Segments of a Contemporary*

Morning. But it is in films that Michael has really made his mark. His first feature film was the Kenny Rogers auto racing movie, *Six Pack*. There was also the hilarious *National Lampoon's Vacation*, where Michael was outstanding as Chevy Chase's son. But it was the three films by John Hughes, America's number one director of teenage movies, that made Michael one of the most familiar young faces in films today. In *Sixteen Candles* he was the nerd pursuing Molly Ringwald. In *The Breakfast Club*, he was a brainy nerd, and in *Weird Science* he was an even brainier one. He was, quite simply, the funniest teenager in films.

But Michael is now eighteen. While he still has a very youthful appearance, he's grown quite tall. He is certainly no longer the cute little boy of *Sixteen Candles*. He wanted to get away from the comic parts he'd played in the past. "I enjoyed acting in comedies, but I knew that I wanted to try something different."

His first straight dramatic role in films was playing Daryl Cage, a rural Iowa teenager who quite innocently gets caught up in a violent and deadly situation. Unfortunately, the film, *Out of Bounds*, was neither a critical nor a popular success. But no actor, no matter how successful, appears only in successful films. Although he has already been acting for a number

Anthony Michael Hall and Jenny Wright in
Out of Bounds
(Photo: Steve Shapiro; © 1986 Columbia Pictures Industries, Inc. All rights reserved. Courtesy of Columbia Pictures)

of years, the very talented Anthony Michael Hall is only at the beginning of his career.

Despite his devotion to the craft of acting, Michael does have another interest—basketball. He's a fanatic basketball fan. "I love making movies, I really do," he said. "Of course, if I could be Larry Bird or Michael Jordan, I'd give it all up today. Movies are fun, but hoops is serious business."

EMILIO ESTEVEZ

Of all the young actors on the scene today, Emilio Estevez knows more about the crazy and sometimes brutal world of entertainment than any other. Emilio is smart, and multi-talented, but having a famous actor for a father and growing up in a show business atmosphere helped, too.

Family connections can give you an advantage in any business, but they are particularly helpful in the highly competitive world of show business. Estevez is the son of actor Martin Sheen. But he decided not to use his father's name professionally. Actually, Estevez is his father's *real* name. Sheen was the name he adopted professionally. So Emilio has really gone back to the original family name. Though the name may not be the same, Emilio strongly resembles his father both physically and in their low-key, yet intense acting styles. Father and son have appeared together on television several times and on the stage once, in a revival of the play *Mister Roberts*. Emilio's acting style is also reminiscent of that of his idol, Jimmy Dean.

Emilio Estevez was born on May 12, 1962, in New York City, but since his father's work took him to Hollywood more and more often, the family moved to Los Angeles when he was quite young. Emilio is very much a California rather than a New York actor.

He never took an acting lesson but, "I've been acting all my life," he says. "Having an actor father is more valuable than anything that can be taught." He started acting and producing shows when he was in second grade. Most of these very youthful productions featured his brothers Roman and Charlie as well as some of the neighborhood kids like Rob and Chad Lowe and Sean and Chris Penn. It wasn't your average neighborhood.

Santa Monica High School wasn't your average high school, either. While still in high school, Emilio began developing another of his talents, writing. He wrote and starred in a play about Vietnam veterans called *Echoes of an Era*. He also acted in a short antinuclear film, *Meet Mr. Bomb*. In high school, Emilio was

Emilio Estevez (right) and father Martin Sheen
(Walter McBride/Retna Ltd.)

really interested in sports. But he figured he'd never make it as a professional athlete, and he had better stick with acting.

Emilio went into acting full time at the age of eighteen, right after his graduation from high school. Almost immediately, he picked up the starring role in a TV after-school special for teenagers called "Seventeen Going on Nowhere."

That started him on what might have become a career of playing hoods and punks. He was Johnny Collins in *The Outsiders* and Two-Bit Matthews in *Tex*. He was also in a film called *Nightmares*. But his most successful punk role was in a weird little low-budget film called *Repo Man*.

Repo Man is a sort of dark comedy, science fiction film. Emilio is a young punker turned auto repossession man, hence the title. It involves a car that has some extraterrestrials locked in the trunk and a government conspiracy and lots of other things. Much of the film simply doesn't make sense. It's not supposed to. It's just very funny. *Repo Man* was never intended for a mass market. But when it came out, it attracted a surprising amount of favorable attention. Though it probably never showed in your neighborhood, it has become a real cult favorite on videocasette. In case you haven't seen it yet, it's well worth a look, and we suspect that it will last longer than some of Emilio's big box office hits.

One of those big hits was *The Breakfast Club,* which not only starred contemporaries like Judd Nelson and Ally Sheedy, but some even younger actors like Molly Ringwald and Anthony Michael Hall. Emilio jumped at the chance to play jock Andy Clark in *The Breakfast Club,* "because I'd never had a chance to play a jock or a model son before. I'd always played hoodlums." No smart actor wants to be typecast.

While taking a screen test for a film to be called *St. Elmo's Fire,* Emilio met a husky-voiced young actress named Demi Moore. They both got parts in the film, and since then have been seen together regularly. According to some sources they are formally engaged.

Along with Estevez and Moore, Rob Lowe, Ally Sheedy, Judd Nelson, and a host of other young actors and actresses were in *St. Elmo's Fire*. It became the quintessential "Brat Pack" film—that, by the way, is a term invented by a writer for *New York* magazine to define this new group of young performers and widely hated and resented by the actors themselves. But whatever you want to call it, *St. Elmo's Fire* was a huge box office success.

Emilio's next film, *That Was Then, This Is Now,* was both a box office and critical failure.

The failure was a double blow for Emilio, for he was not only the star of the film, he also wrote the screenplay, based on the S.E. Hinton novel of the same name. Emilio still regards Mark, the part he played in *That Was Then,* as his best role to date. But he hasn't allowed the failure to discourage or embitter him. He grew up with acting and he knows the ups and downs of the life. "This is my profession and I'm gonna do the best job I can. Forget about everything else."

"The idea," he explains, "is to have the next project negotiated before this one opens up."

Emilio had no trouble finding that next project. It was *Maximum Overdrive,* a film based on a Stephen King novel that was also directed by the king of the terror novel himself.

In a sense, *Maximum Overdrive* was just a momentary diversion for Emilio; it was the next film that he was really interested in. The film is called *Wisdom,* about a Robin Hood type of bank robber who gives the money that he steals to the needy. Emilio not only has the starring role, he also wrote the film, and directs it as well. That sort of virtuoso performance is always risky for actors. They can lose perspective on their work. In addition, Emilio has cast Demi Moore as his sidekick, and there is even a cameo appearance by Emilio's younger brother, Chris Sheen, as the boss of a fast-food joint. As of this writing, we don't know how *Wisdom* will fare.

But win or lose, Emilio already has that next project lined up. He's set to direct a dark comedy about a couple of L.A. garbagemen who find a dead body.

As we said, of all the young actors and actresses on the Hollywood scene today, Emilio Estevez probably has the best grasp of the moviemaking business. Why shouldn't he? It's the business that he grew up with, and he's going to make the most of it.

ALYSSA MILANO

Thirteen-year-old Alyssa Milano had a good start in show business. She had the support and guidance of a street-wise New York family. Her father, Tom, is a music coordinator. Her mother, Lin, is a fashion designer.

Alyssa was born in Brooklyn and raised on Staten Island, New York. She had been studying dance and dreaming of a show business career from the age of four. At the age of eight she saw the musical *Annie* on stage and, like millions of other young girls, decided that she wanted a part in that show. When auditions opened up for a touring company of *Annie,* she showed up and won a part as one of the orphans. Though Alyssa's family knew something about show business, they had no special connections. She won her part at an open audition,

Alyssa Milano
(Courtesy Ryder Public Relations)

crammed with girls all dreaming of a career on stage. Alyssa succeeded on her own and she's very proud of that accomplishment. "Of over 1,500 children who auditioned for parts in *Annie,* four were finally chosen for roles and I was one of them."

Her next stage role was as Adelle in a musical adaptation of the novel *Jane Eyre*. Then there were a couple of other serious roles in off-Broadway shows. By the age of ten, Alyssa Jayne Milano was a seasoned trooper. And that was just the start. Her first feature film role was in *Old Enough,* which picked up awards at the prestigious Cannes Film Festival in France.

Her next big break came when she auditioned for the part of Tony Danza's daughter, Samantha, in the TV series "Who's the Boss?" When the part opened up, it seemed as if every young actress in Hollywood went out for it. But it was Alyssa who came away with the prize, and the show has been a major hit.

From playing Tony Danza's daughter, Alyssa went to playing Arnold Schwarzenegger's daughter in the film *Commando,* one of the big hits of the summer of '85. When filming a made-for-TV movie, *Canterville Ghost,* in England, Alyssa got to work with a very different sort of costar, the great British actor Sir John Gielgud.

All-in-all, fame has come very quickly to

Alyssa Milano

Alyssa. She recently won the Youth Film Awards "Best Young Supporting Actress in a TV Series" and is "Spokeswoman" for a leading brand of teenage clothes.

How does she handle all the fame at such a young age? "I handle it day by day," she told the *Los Angeles Times*. "Just how it comes. I don't think fame has changed my life. If so, I hope it's for the better."

She also told the *Times* that the hardest thing about her career is the fact that she still has to do schoolwork. That shouldn't come as a big surprise to many of you. "I'm an A-minus student. I'm especially good in French. I'm not very good in math, but it's my favorite subject. I like working with numbers.

"I have a tutor on the set. I have to do school three hours a day. That's a requirement. I have to study 16 hours a week."

Unlike the tomboy character of Samantha that she plays on "Who's the Boss?," Alyssa says that she hates sports.

Alyssa is quite specific when asked how much work she puts in on the set. It's four days a week of rehearsals and a full day of taping on Friday. What she particularly likes about the show is that it's taped before a live audience, so there is some immediate feedback. "In a movie, you must wait until it is released before you get a response."

Alyssa Milano and John Gielgud in *The Canterville Ghost*
(Courtesy Ryder Public Relations)

When asked by the Long Island paper *Newsday* how much money she makes, she wouldn't be so specific. All she said was, "A lot." But all the money isn't turned over directly to her. "Forty percent of the money goes to a trust fund and when I turn eighteen I get to have it all."

Alyssa Milano

Unlike a lot of today's young stars, Alyssa never did many commercials. "When I used to go for commercials, I wouldn't get the parts because I was very ethnic looking. I was darker and very Italian looking." Hardly surprising, since she is Italian, and very proud of it.

Alyssa hopes to continue acting. "My biggest goal is that I want to be a successful actress known for comedy and drama." But she has some wider goals as well. She wants to write screenplays and direct. These goals are not pipe dreams. Some of the money that she is now earning is being set aside for college. She wants to attend the film school at UCLA.

Alyssa is a bit uncomfortable with the label of Teen Idol, though she admits that she gets a lot of fan mail, mostly from boys. But she's an idol in another way, an idol for all the teens and preteens out there who have dreamed of being on stage or on television. What's her advice?

"I was always a ham. I always performed in front of people. I like making people laugh. My advice to any kid who wants to act is just go for it. You never know until you try."

SCOTT GRIMES

Scott Grimes never planned to be an actor. Oh, he liked acting well enough, but he never took it all that seriously. Of course, how seriously does a kid take anything when he is only nine (Scott was born July 9, 1971). That was his age when Scott auditioned for a part in a community theater production of the musical *Oliver!* in his native Lowell, Massachusetts. He won the part, and so much praise from his director, that he and his parents were encouraged to take off for New York, so that he could audition for a Broadway show.

Now here is the amazing part, because there are thousands upon thousands of hopeful families who take their kids to Broadway auditions year after year. Two days after landing in New York, Scott had won the role of Pepe in *Nine,* a

Scott Grimes
(Courtesy Ryder Public Relations)

new musical directed by Tommy Tune, one of Broadway's best musical directors. The production won a Tony for Best Musical, and Scott, in his first professional stage role, entertained tough Broadway audiences for ten months. Talk about getting a career off to a fast start!

He was next offered a role opposite Anthony Newley in the stage premiere of *Chaplin,* a musical based on the life of the great silent film comedian. The show began its run in Los Angeles, but faded before it hit Broadway. Scott's career, however, hardly missed a step. He was next introduced to television, first playing Art Carney's grandson in the TV-movie *Doctor's Story.* Working with another show business legend, Mickey Rooney, Scott was then featured in the movie-of-the-week, *It Came Upon a Midnight Clear.* A Christmas movie, as you can tell from the title.

His first guest starring role came on the series "Hotel," and then it was on to another Christmas special, "The Night They Saved Christmas." With all those Christmas shows over, Scott's career came to a grinding halt—for a whole two months. Then it was back on stage to star with Len Cariou in the production *Traveler in the Dark.*

Scott has made more than his share of appearances at charity benefits for such causes as the USO, the American Cancer Society, and the AIDS Research Foundation. At one AIDS benefit, hosted by Elizabeth Taylor and Bob Hope, Scott so impressed Hope with his singing that the veteran comedian asked Scott to accompany him at a command performance for the king and queen of Sweden at the palace in Stockholm.

Scott arrived in Sweden at a tragic moment. "It was right after the prime minister was killed. We rode down the street in a limo and looked out at thousands and thousands of people throwing flowers. It was weird . . . It was from the respect they have for their country."

Scott's first feature film was the very popular comedy-horror film *Critters*. There was a guest spot on "Who's the Boss?" as Alyssa Milano's boyfriend (the two actually live down the street from each other in Los Angeles), and a starring role in an episode of "The Twilight Zone."

It seemed only a matter of time until Scott Grimes got a starring role in a TV series. That happened in the fall of '86. The show is "Together We Stand" with Elliot Gould and Dee Wallace. At this moment we don't know if the show will be a hit or not. But whatever happens, Scott Grimes has lots of plans for the future. He's already proved himself a talented singer, and might do a Broadway musical again if the right part came along. He's also terribly interested in movies, not only starring in them, but making them as well. His idol is Steven Spielberg. You can't aim much higher than that.

THE COSBY KIDS

Lisa Bonet

Denise may be getting ready to move out of the Huxtable house. Though all the Cosby kids have become famous from their appearances on the incredibly popular "Cosby Show," the character of Denise, played by Lisa Bonet, seems to be the one that has established her individuality most firmly in the public's mind. Lisa's own cool good looks and funky sense of style helped a lot, too.

Now don't get us wrong. There is no trouble and dissension on the Cosby set. It's just that the Denise character has become so popular that "The Cosby Show" producers are thinking of giving Lisa her own spin-off show. In the show, Denise may go off to college in California.

Actually, the Huxtable family already has a daughter away at college. She's Sondra, played

Lisa Bonet
(Barry Taresnik/Retna Ltd.)

by actress Sabrina LeBeauf. She has not played a major part in the show to date.

Otherwise, Lisa is signed on for the duration of "The Cosby Show." Given the show's popularity, that may be a very long time indeed. However, Lisa Bonet is not Denise Huxtable, she's an actress. Happy as she is with the show, she's also got her own future career to think about. For Lisa, there very definitely is life beyond "The Cosby Show," and even beyond her possible spin-off. She's also developing plans for a film in which she will costar with the great actor Robert DeNiro.

Success has come very quickly for Lisa Bonet. She was born November 16, 1967, in San Francisco, California. She is an only child and her mother, a grammar-school teacher, was a single parent from the time Lisa was an infant.

Lisa had wanted to be an actress from an early age. She had studied at the Celluloid Actors Studio in North Hollywood and she had a few small parts before "The Cosby Show" came along. While she was going to Birmingham High School in Van Nuys, California, she hoped she would become an actress. Though Lisa is a confident young lady, she was far from sure that she was going to make it in acting.

In fact, up until the time she landed the part of Denise, she was toying with the idea of giving up acting and going into medicine. It wasn't that she didn't want to be an actress anymore, it's just that her future in acting was looking bleak. In California producers hire a lot of five-foot-eight blondes. Lisa is five feet two and black. She told reporter Aimee Lee Ball, "I watched my friends go on four interviews a day, and I was going on four interviews every six months. I didn't even consider myself an actress."

Then she was called East to audition for "The Cosby Show." At first she was sure that she wasn't going to get the part because she was wearing braces. But when she was called in and told that she had the part, Bill Cosby himself said to her, "I love the braces. Those things are staying on."

So the braces, instead of hurting her, actually helped her get the job. Another thing that helped is the funky and unpredictable way that she dressed. That characteristic has been carried over from the real Lisa to the fictional Denise. The manner of dress has also helped to define the character of Denise as the most independent and unpredictable of the Cosby kids.

Lisa admits to being a "clothesaholic." Once, while some of the cast members were doing a promotion at a big department store in Paramus, New Jersey, so many fans turned up that the store's security force couldn't handle the crowd. Cast members were warned to stay in one place and not mingle with the crowd. They all did as told except Lisa. She was in a store, and she couldn't stop herself. Despite the dangers, she went shopping anyway.

Though Lisa still lives in Reseda, California

with her mother, she spends a lot of time in the East. "The Cosby Show" is filmed in Brooklyn. She admits that she misses the Pacific Ocean and the California sun. But she has also learned that fame changes your life and it sometimes changes the attitudes of the people you know.

She went back home to California for her high school graduation. She wasn't really graduating, since she had already completed her high school work with the aid of tutors furnished by the show's producer. Lisa just wanted to celebrate with her friends. Then she discovered that a lot of them weren't her friends anymore. Her newfound fame had come between them.

There are, however, compensations. When Lisa appeared on "Night of 100 Stars," she had people like Michael Caine and Gregory Hines come up to her and tell her that she was one of *their* favorite actresses.

"Before it was like we were more like fans of stars than colleagues. Now we can be having dinner with Anthony Quinn and we're like, on the same level. It's real neat."

Malcolm-Jamal Warner

Even if you're a star, if you're seventeen years old, there are still things that you must do.

Malcolm-Jamal Warner
(Courtesy Pamela Warner)

When Malcolm-Jamal Warner goes home, his attractive and strong-willed mother Pamela still insists that he make his own bed.

Another thing his mother insists on is that he keep his grades up. "If my grades ever slip, no more acting until the grades come back up and stay there," says Malcolm. It's a pact he made with his mother.

With the demands of taping a weekly TV show, Malcolm can't go to a regular school. Like most very young actors on television series, he has tutors on the set. He shared his tutors with Lisa Bonet, until she "graduated." A lot of young actors say that they miss regular school and their friends in the classroom. Not so Malcolm. He finds working with tutors a lot easier.

"It's easier for me because there are fewer students, and I can have the pace adjusted to suit my own needs." He misses his friends from school, but he admits that if he were in a regular classroom he would probably be one of those students the teacher always has to ask to be quiet.

Malcolm-Jamal Warner was born on March 16, 1970, in Jersey City, New Jersey. Like Lisa Bonet, he's an only child. After he moved to Los Angeles with his mother in 1975, he was bitten by the acting bug. Pam Warner was looking for some wholesome outside activity for her son. Through casual conversation, she heard about a local theater group and that's how Malcolm's career started. He first appeared in some local stage productions, and his performance attracted the attention of some talent agents. It wasn't long before he was picking up parts on TV shows like "Fame," Call to Glory," and "Matt Houston."

The Cosby Kids

However, it was "The Cosby Show" that changed his life. Now he can't even walk down the street without being noticed. Fans always stop him and ask him for an autograph. "It's a great way to meet girls," he admits.

Malcolm does not have any firm plans for the future yet. He wants to continue in acting, and he wants to grow and perfect his abilities. But he does admit that his first love is still basketball. "My idols are the L.A. Lakers."

Tempestt Bledsoe

When Tempestt Bledsoe was only four years old, her mother decided that all her abundant energy should be put into something constructive. Tempestt was also a very attractive child. So her mother figured she might be a good child model. In less than a year Tempestt began getting regular modeling jobs.

After that it was television. There were no shows, no acting, but there were commercials, including some big ones like McDonald's when she was only eight.

Commercials are one thing, a show, particularly one starring someone as well known as Bill Cosby, was something else again. Tempestt's agent asked her if she wanted to audition, and Tempestt says she was "over-

"The Cosby Show" *(top, l.-r.)* Sabrina LeBeauf, Tempestt Bledsoe, Malcolm-Jamal Warner; *(front, l.-r.)* Lisa Bonet, Bill Cosby, Keshia Knight Pulliam, Phylicia Rashad.

(© 1986 National Broadcasting Co.)

whelmed" by the opportunity. The part didn't just fall into her lap. In the first place, the show's producers weren't sure if they wanted the character to be a boy or girl. There was a whole series of callbacks, and then a final audition before some network executives and Bill Cosby himself. Up to that point there was another girl and a guy still in the running. Tempestt got the part. The only bad thing about the show, from Tempestt's point of view, is that she has had to move from Chicago, where she was born, and a city that she loves, to New York, where the show is produced. "I like Chicago better because my friends are there."

By now, of course, she has lots of new friends in New York, and everywhere else in the U.S. and indeed around the world, everywhere "The Cosby Show" is seen.

Keshia Knight Pulliam

If you become a star when you are only six years old, it figures that you started in show business pretty early. Keshia Knight Pulliam, who plays Rudy, the baby of the Huxtable family, started her career when she was only eight months old. She appeared in a diaper commercial. After that it was on to bigger things, like "Sesame Street." She also appeared in a film,

The Last Dragon. As a matter of fact, the youngest of the Cosby kids probably had more experience in show business before the series began than any of her television brothers and sisters.

Keshia was born on April 9th, 1979, in Newark, New Jersey. Her family has remained in New Jersey, now living in the suburb of Irvington.

"The Cosby Show" made Keshia a major star before she was six years old. There is every indication that the enormously popular show will run for years. And after that there are reruns, and, of course, with the reruns come residuals, that is, money. It's a safe bet that Keshia is pretty well fixed financially for a very long time to come. What are her career plans? Well, she's a bit too young to have any firm plans yet, but since she's been in show business for almost all of her life, we would be willing to bet that she'll want to stick with it.

YOUNG STARS FROM BRITAIN

If you're a real film buff, you might have noticed something. British films are coming back. The American film industry, centered in Hollywood, has always been number one. But for a long time the British were second. They had a thriving film industry. But things have not gone well in Britain for a number of years now. By the mid 1960s, it seemed as if the entire British film industry was going to collapse. Then suddenly, over the last couple of years, the British have started making movies again.

The movies now being made in Britain are very different from those being made in the United States. They are very low-budget. British producers can make ten or fifteen films for the price of one cheap Hollywood movie. The British films are exported to America. Usually, they are not widely distributed, only showing up in a few movie houses in the larger cities. But even so, these films make money because they cost so little to produce.

These new British films are developing a whole host of new young British stars. They have been dubbed "the Brit Pack," a spin-off from the American term "Brat Pack." You probably have not seen or even heard of these new young stars—yet. But the film industry is really international. Chances are that you will be hearing about some of them soon.

Helena Bonham Carter

Helena Bonham Carter doesn't come from a theatrical family, but she does come from a family that is both wealthy and distinguished. She is the great granddaughter of Lord Asquith, who was once prime minister of England, and the granddaughter of a famous member of the House of Lords, Lady Violet Bonham Carter. Her father was a merchant banker, her mother a psychotherapist.

Helena seemed destined to go to a good university to study English or philosophy. But she had different ideas. She won some money in a contest for young writers. She then used the money to buy an ad in a casting directory.

Helena Bonham Carter
(Ian McKell/Retna Ltd.)

Though she had absolutely no previous training or experience, an agent liked her looks and admired her pluck, so he took the teenager on as a client.

Helena's first role was appropriate for her aristocratic background. She played the tragic Lady Jane Grey who briefly held the throne of England after the death of Henry VIII. The film was called *Lady Jane*. The historical Lady Jane was sixteen, Helena was eighteen when the picture was shot. There had been talk that the unknown actress only got the part because of her famous ancestors. This would assure that the picture would get lots of publicity, but that the untrained upstart couldn't act. All of that sort of talk stopped when *Lady Jane* was released. The film is full of castles and costumes. Some of the critics found it slow, even silly. But there was almost universal praise for Helena. She played the doomed and unworldly Lady Jane with believability and great skill. Her acting career was well launched.

A lot of attention has been paid to Helena's looks. She is very pretty. She is also extremely intelligent. All the talk about her appearance makes her uncomfortable. She thinks that if you are simply looked upon as pretty, then people don't take you seriously. She doesn't even like the word *actress*. She finds that it has "overtones of glamour and stresses the female bit rather than the acting."

Helena's second film, *A Room With a View,* is set in romantic, turn-of-the century Italy and England. This film was well received in art houses in the United States. Once again there were raves for Helena. The character she plays is supposed to be a rather silly young lady, and some critics pointed out that she doesn't act quite silly enough. The real Helena is too bright and too much in control. She doesn't entirely succeed in covering that up.

Helena is probably her own harshest critic. She feels she needs more acting training and perhaps more education. "At the moment I don't have much to impart to the world, and I wish this attention would come at a time when I did," she told *Time* magazine.

Daniel Day Lewis

The fellow who plays Helena's twit fiance in *A Room With a View* is Daniel Day Lewis. He's also attracting rave reviews both in Britain and in the U.S. Like Helena, he comes from a distinguished family. He's the son of Cecil Day Lewis, once poet laureate of England. Although there's nothing like that in America, to be poet laureate is a great honor in England and means being sort of the country's official poet.

Daniel got his start on the stage, and live theater remains his first love. He's turned down a flock of tempting offers from Hollywood to work for comparatively low pay in Britain's National Theatre.

Daniel hasn't totally turned his back on films, however. He was brilliant as a working-class punk in a film with the strange title of *My Beautiful Laundrette*.

Daniel does not like to think of himself as a star; he is devoted to the craft of acting. He has not let all the praise and all the offers go to his head. Friends describe him as being "Totally unspoilt and disgustingly handsome."

Margi Clark and Alexandra Pigg

Liverpool is the grimy working-class city in England that was the home of the Beatles and lots of other rock groups. Since the time of the Beatles, Liverpool, which was never rich, has gotten even poorer. But the poverty hasn't crushed the creative spirit. A group of unemployed Liverpool young people got together, pooled what little money they had, and began shooting a film. Finally they managed to get a

Young Stars from Britain

grant from one of Britian's TV stations which often backs films.

The result was a tough and touching comedy-romance called *Letter to Brezhnev*. Stars of the film were Margi Clarke and Alexandra Pigg (there's a name for you), playing a couple of working-class Liverpool girls, which is what they really are. Alexandra is the daughter of an unemployed cook, Margi is one of ten children in the family of a night watchman.

Letter to Brezhnev amazed American filmmakers, not only because it was so good, but because it was so cheap to make. "I think anyone who needs $30 million to make a movie is insane," says Margi.

These are just four members of the so-called "Brit Pack." There are many others. It's another indication that all around the world there is a whole new generation of rising young stars.

About the Authors

DANIEL COHEN is the author of over a hundred books for both young readers and adults, including some titles he has co-authored with his wife SUSAN. Among their popular titles are: *Supermonsters; The Greatest Monsters in the World; Real Ghosts; Ghostly Terrors; Science Fiction's Greatest Monsters; The World's Most Famous Ghosts; Heroes of the Challenger; Rock Video Superstars; Rock Video Superstars II; Wrestling Superstars; Wrestling Superstars II;* and *The Monsters of Star Trek;* all of which are available in Archway Paperback editions.

A former managing editor of *Science Digest* magazine, Mr. Cohen was born in Chicago and has a degree in journalism from the University of Illinois. He appears frequently on radio and television and has lectured at colleges and universities throughout the country. He lives with his wife, young daughter, one dog, and four cats in Port Jervis, New York.

**Fast-paced, action-packed stories—
the ultimate adventure/mystery series!**

COMING SOON...
HAVE YOU SEEN
THE HARDY BOYS LATELY?

Beginning in April 1987, all-new Hardy Boys mysteries will be available in pocket-sized editions called THE HARDY BOYS CASEFILES.

Frank and Joe Hardy are eighties guys with eighties interests, living in Bayport, U.S.A. Their extracurricular activities include girlfriends, fast-food joints, hanging out at the mall and quad theaters. But computer whiz Frank and the charming, athletic Joe are deep into international intrigue and high-tech drama. The pace of these mysteries just never lets up!

For a sample of the *new* Hardy Boys, turn the page and enjoy excerpts from DEAD ON TARGET and EVIL, INC., the first two books in THE HARDY BOYS CASEFILES.

And don't forget to look for more of the new Hardy Boys and details about a great Hardy Boys contest in April!

THE HARDY BOYS CASEFILES™

Case #1
Dead on Target

A terrorist bombing sends Frank and Joe on a mission of revenge.

"GET OUT OF my way, Frank!" Joe Hardy shoved past his brother, shouting to be heard over the roar of the flames. Straight ahead, a huge fireball rose like a mushroom cloud over the parking lot. Flames shot fifty feet into the air, dropping chunks of wreckage—wreckage that just a moment earlier had been their yellow sedan. "Iola's in there! We've got to get her out!"

Frank stared, his lean face frozen in shock, as his younger brother ran straight for the billowing flames. Then he raced after Joe, catching him in a flying tackle twenty feet away from the blaze. Even at that distance they could feel the heat.

"Do you want to get yourself killed?" Frank yelled, rising to his knees.

Joe remained silent, his blue eyes staring at the wall of flame, his blond hair mussed by the fall.

Frank hauled his brother around, making Joe face him. "She wouldn't have lasted a second," he said, trying to soften the blow. "Face it, Joe."

For an instant, Frank thought the message had gotten through. Joe sagged against the concrete. Then he surged up again, eyes wild. "No! I can save her! Let go!"

Before Joe could get to his feet, Frank tackled him again, sending both of them tumbling along the ground. Joe began struggling, thrashing against his brother's grip. With near-maniacal strength, he broke Frank's hold, then started throwing wild punches at his brother, almost as if he were grateful to have a physical enemy to attack.

Frank blocked the flailing blows, lunging forward to grab Joe again. But a fist pounded through his guard, catching him full in the mouth. Frank flopped on his back, stunned, as his brother lurched to his feet and staggered toward the inferno.

Painfully pulling himself up, Frank wiped something wet from his lips—blood. He sprinted after Joe, blindly snatching at his T-shirt. The fabric tore loose in his hand.

Forcing himself farther into the glare and suffocating heat, Frank managed to get a grip on his brother's arm. Joe didn't even try to shake free. He just pulled both of them closer to the flames.

The air was so hot it scorched Frank's throat as he gasped for breath. He flipped Joe free, throwing him off balance. Then he wrapped one arm around Joe's neck and cocked the other back, flashing in a karate blow. Joe went limp in his brother's arms.

As Frank dragged them both out of danger, he heard the wail of sirens in the distance. We should never have come, he thought, never.

Just an hour before, Joe had jammed the brakes on the car, stopping in front of the mall. "So *this* is why we had to come here," he exclaimed. "They're having a rally! Give me a break, Iola."

"You knew we were working on the campaign." Iola grinned, looking like a little dark-haired pixie. "Would you have come if we'd told you?"

"No way! What do you think, we're going to stand around handing out Walker for President buttons?" Joe scowled at his girlfriend.

"Actually, they're leaflets," Callie Shaw said from the backseat. She leaned forward to peer at herself in the rearview mirror and ran her fingers hastily through her short brown hair.

"So that's what you've got stuck between us!" Frank rapped the cardboard box on the seat.

"I thought you liked Walker," said Callie.

"He's all right," Frank admitted. "He looked good on TV last night, saying we should fight back against terrorists. At least he's not a wimp."

"That antiterrorism thing has gotten a lot of coverage," Iola said. "Besides . . ."

". . . He's cute," Frank cut in, mimicking Iola.

"The most gorgeous politician I've ever seen."

Laughter cleared the air as they pulled into a parking space. "Look, we're not really into passing out pamphlets—or leaflets, or whatever they are," Frank said. "But we will do something to help. We'll beef up your crowd."

"Yeah," Joe grumbled. "It sounds like a real hot afternoon."

The mall was a favorite hangout for Bayport kids—three floors with more than a hundred stores arranged around a huge central well. The Saturday sunshine streamed down from the glass roof to ground level—the Food Floor. But that day, instead of the usual tables for pizzas, burgers, and burritos, the space had been cleared out, except for a band, which was tuning up noisily.

The music blasted up to the roof, echoing in the huge open space. Heads began appearing, staring down, along the safety railings that lined the shopping levels. Still more shoppers gathered on the Food Floor. Callie, Iola, and four other kids circulated through the crowd, handing out leaflets.

The Food Floor was packed with people cheering and applauding. But Frank Hardy backed away, turned off by all the hype. Since he'd lost Joe after about five seconds in the jostling mob, he fought his way to the edges of the crowd, trying to spot him.

Joe was leaning against one of the many pillars supporting the mall. He had a big grin on his face and was talking with a gorgeous blond girl. Frank hurried over to them. But Joe, deep in conversation with his new friend, didn't notice his brother. More importantly, he didn't notice his girlfriend making her way through the crowd.

Frank arrived about two steps behind Iola, who had wrapped one arm around Joe's waist while glaring at the blond. "Oh, uh, hi," said Joe, his grin fading in embarrassment. "This is Val. She just came—"

"I'd love to stay and talk," Iola said, cutting Joe off, "but we have a problem. We're running out of leaflets. The only ones left are on the backseat of your car. Could you help me get them?"

"Right now? We just got here," Joe complained.

"Yeah, and I can see you're really busy," Iola said, looking at Val. "Are you coming?"

Joe hesitated for a moment, looking from Iola to the blond girl. "Okay." His hand fished around in his pocket and came out with his car keys. "I'll be with you in a minute, okay?" He started playing catch with the keys, tossing them in the air as he turned back to Val.

But Iola angrily snatched the keys in midair. Then she rushed off, nearly knocking Frank over.

"Hey, Joe, I've got to talk to you," Frank said, smiling at Val as he took his brother by the elbow. "Excuse us a second." He pulled Joe around the pillar.

"What's going on?" Joe complained. "I can't even start a friendly conversation without everybody jumping on me."

"You know, it's lucky you're so good at picking up girls," said Frank. "Because you sure are tough on the ones you already know."

Joe's face went red. "What are you talking about?"

"You know what I'm talking about. I saw your little trick with the keys there a minute ago. You made Iola look like a real jerk in front of some girl you've been hitting on. Make up your mind, Joe. Is Iola your girlfriend or not?"

Joe seemed to be studying the toes of his running shoes as Frank spoke. "You're right, I guess," he finally muttered. "But I was gonna go! Why did she have to make such a life-and-death deal out of it?"

Frank grinned. "It's your fatal charm, Joe. It stirs up women's passions."

"Very funny." Joe sighed. "So what should I do?"

"Let's go out to the car and give Iola a hand," Frank suggested. "She can't handle that big box all by herself."

He put his head around the pillar and smiled at Val. "Sorry. I have to borrow this guy for a while. We'll be back in a few minutes."

They headed for the nearest exit. The sleek, modern mall decor gave way to painted cinderblocks as they headed down the corridor to the underground parking garages. "We should've caught up to her by now," Joe said as they came to the first row of cars. "She must be really steamed."

He was glancing around for Iola, but the underground lot was a perfect place for hide-and-seek. Every ten feet or so, squat concrete pillars which supported the upper levels rose from the floor, blocking the view. But as the Hardys reached the end of the row of cars, they saw a dark-haired figure marching angrily ahead of them.

"Iola!" Joe called.

Instead of turning around, Iola put on speed.

"Hey, Iola, wait a minute!" Joe picked up his pace, but Iola darted around a pillar. A second later she'd disappeared.

"Calm down," Frank said. "She'll be outside at the car. You can talk to her then."

Joe led the way to the outdoor parking lot, nervously pacing ahead of Frank. "She's really angry," he said as they stepped outside. "I just hope she doesn't—"

The explosion drowned out whatever he was going to say. They ran to the spot where they'd parked their yellow sedan. But the car—and Iola—had erupted in a ball of white-hot flame!

Case #2
Evil, Inc.

When Frank and Joe take on Reynard and Company, they find that murder is business as usual.

THE FRENCH POLICE officer kept his eyes on the two teenagers from the moment they sat down at the outdoor café across the street from the Pompidou Center in Paris.

Those two kids spelled trouble. The cop knew their type. *Les punks* was what the French called them. Both of them had spiky hair; one had dyed his jet black, the other bright green. They wore identical black T-shirts emblazoned with the words *The Poison Pens* in brilliant yellow, doubtless some unpleasant rock group. Their battered, skintight black trousers seemed ready to split at the seams. And their scuffed black leather combat boots looked as if they had gone through a couple of wars. A gold earring gleamed on one earlobe of each boy.

What were they waiting for? the cop wondered. Somebody to mug? Somebody to sell drugs to? He was sure of one thing: the punks were up to no good as they sat waiting and watchful at their table, nursing tiny cups of black coffee. True, one of them looked very interested in any pretty girl who passed by. But when a couple of girls stopped in front of the table, willing to be friendly, the second punk said something sharp to the first, who shrugged a silent apology to the girls. The girls shrugged back and went on their way, leaving the two punks to scan the passing crowd.

The cop wished he could hear their conversation and find out what language they spoke. You couldn't tell kids' nationalities nowadays by their appearance. Teen styles crossed all boundaries, he had decided.

If the cop had been able to hear the two boys, he would have known instantly where they were from.

"Cool it. This is no time to play Casanova," one of them said.

"Aw, come on," the other answered. "So many girls—so little time."

Their voices were as American as apple pie, even if their appearances weren't.

In fact, their voices were the only things about them that even their closest friends back home would have recognized.

"Let's keep our minds on the job," Frank Hardy told his brother.

"Remember what they say about all work and no play," Joe Hardy answered.

"And *you* remember that if we make one wrong move here in Paris," Frank said, "it'll be our last."

Sitting in the summer late-afternoon sunlight at the Café des Nations, Frank was having a hard time keeping Joe's mind on business. He had no sooner made Joe break off a budding friendship with two pretty girls who had stopped in front of their table, when another one appeared. One look at her, and Frank knew that Joe would be hard to discourage.

She looked about eighteen years old. Her pale complexion was flawless and untouched by makeup except for dark shading around her green eyes. Her hair was flaming red, and if it was dyed, it was very well done. She wore a white T-shirt that showed off her slim figure, faded blue jeans that hugged her legs down to her bare ankles, and high-heeled sandals. Joe didn't have to utter a word to say what he thought of her. His eyes said it all: Gorgeous!

Even Frank wasn't exactly eager to get rid of her.

Especially when she leaned toward them, gave them a smile, and said, "Brother, can you spare a million?"

"Sit down," Joe said instantly.

But the girl remained standing. Her gaze flicked toward the policeman who stood watching them.

"Too hot out here in the sun," she said with the faintest of French accents. "I know someplace that's cooler. Come on."

Frank left some change on the table to pay for the coffees, then he and Joe hurried off with the girl.

"What's your name?" Joe asked.

"Denise," she replied. "And which brother are you, Joe or Frank?"

"I'm Joe," Joe said. "The handsome, charming one."

"Where are we going?" asked Frank.

"And that's Frank," Joe added. "The dull, businesslike one."

"Speaking of business," said Denise, "do you have the money?"

"Do you have the goods?" asked Frank.

"*Trust* the young lady," Joe said, putting his arm around her shoulder. "Anyone who looks as good as she does can't be bad."

"First, you answer," Denise said to Frank.

"I've got the money," said Frank.

"Then I've got the goods," said Denise.

The Hardys and Denise were walking through a maze of twisting streets behind the Pompidou Center. Denise glanced over her shoulder each time they turned, making sure they weren't being followed. Finally she seemed satisfied.

"In here," she said, indicating the entranceway to a grime-covered old building.

They entered a dark hallway, and Denise flicked a switch.

"We have to hurry up the stairs," she said. "The light stays on for just sixty seconds."

At the top of the creaking stairs was a steel door, which clearly had been installed to discourage thieves. Denise rapped loudly on it: four raps, a pause, and then two more.

The Hardys heard the sound of a bolt being unfastened and then a voice saying, *"Entrez."*

Denise swung the door open and motioned for Frank and Joe to go in first.

They did.

A man was waiting for them in the center of a shabbily furnished room.

Neither Frank nor Joe could have said what he looked like.

All they could see was what was in his hand.

It was a pistol—and it was pointed directly at them.

And don't miss these other exciting all-new adventures in THE HARDY BOYS CASEFILES

Case #3
Cult of Crime

High in the untamed Adirondack Mountains lurks one of the most fiendish plots Frank and Joe Hardy have ever encountered. On a mission to rescue their good friend Holly from the cult of the lunatic Rajah, the boys unwittingly become the main event in one of the madman's deadly rituals—human sacrifice.

Fleeing from gun-wielding "religious" zealots and riding a danger-infested train through the wilderness, Frank and Joe arrive home to find the worst has happened. The Rajah and his followers have invaded Bayport. As their hometown is about to go up in flames, the boys look to Holly for help. But Holly has plans of her own, and one deadly secret.

Available in May 1987.

Case #4
The Lazarus Plot

Camped out in the Maine woods, the Hardy boys get a real jolt when they glimpse Joe's old girlfriend, Iola Morton. Can it really be the same girl who was blown to bits before their eyes by a terrorist bomb? Frantically searching for her, Frank and Joe are trapped in the lair of the most diabolical team of scientists ever assembled.

Twisting technology to their own ends, the criminals create perfect replicas of the boys. Now the survival of a top-secret government intelligence organization is at stake. Frank and Joe must discover the bizarre truth about Iola and face their doubles alone—before the scientists unleash one final, deadly experiment.

Available in June 1987.

HAVE YOU SEEN THE HARDY BOYS® LATELY?

Bond has high-tech equipment, Indiana Jones courage and daring...

ONLY THE *HARDY BOYS CASE FILES* HAVE IT ALL!!

Now you can continue to enjoy the Hardy Boys in a new action-packed series written especially for older readers. Each pocket-sized paperback has more high-tech adventure, intrigue, mystery and danger than ever before.

In the new Hardy Boys Case Files series, Frank and Joe pursue one thrilling adventure after another. With their intelligence, charm, knowledge of the martial arts and their state-of-the-art equipment, the Hardys find themselves investigating international terrorism, espionage rings, religious cults, and crime families. Whether they're in Europe or Bayport, The Hardy Boys® are never far from life-or-death action.

THE HARDY BOYS CASE FILES	#1 DEAD ON TARGET #2 EVIL, INC.

AVAILABLE IN APRIL

Archway Paperbacks
Published by Pocket Books,
A Division of Simon & Schuster, Inc.